I0743154

THE MARCHING BAND EMPORIUM

A PERSONAL SELECTION

L.A. DAVENPORT

Copyright © 2012 by L.A. Davenport

All rights reserved.

No part of this book may be reproduced in any form or by any electronic or mechanical means, including information storage and retrieval systems, without written permission from the author, except for the use of brief quotations in a book review.

Illustration Copyright © 2019 by L.A. Davenport.

CONTENTS

Preface   v
Introduction   vii
Note   ix

Excerpts from lost novels   1
Together   5
Another living room   6
Dream   7
Excerpts from lost novels   9
Shattered—a mini saga   12
Drink, drink up, my friends   13
Dancer   15
Excerpts from lost novels   16
An artistic death—a mini saga   19
The interview   20
Sometimes   23
Curled Up   26
Excerpts from lost novels   27
Morning   30
Socrates in the dust   32
Just a joke   35
View of Place des Arcades, Antibes, France   39
Excerpts from lost novels   40
The rush of life—a mini saga   43
Test your intelligence!   44
Excerpts from lost novels   47
Fort Carre, Antibes, France   50

THE CANCER WITHIN
Part I   53
Part II   57
Final Part   61

After hearing yet another discussion of Dante's Inferno	68
Excerpts from lost novels	69
The box	72
Marty the dapper wolf	75
Is this love?	76
Prisons	79
Excerpts from lost novels	81
The other Luther	85
Shadow of me	88
Every day—a mini saga	89
Manhole	90
The station	93
Excerpts from lost novels	95
Watching, waiting	98
A double romance	99
The empty attic—a mini saga	103
The rain	104
Excerpts from lost novels	107
Candid Café, Islington, London	111

THE ELECTRIC LOVE STORY
Yes Please!	115
Plastic Heartbreak	119
Feel Me	123

Excerpts from lost novels	128
The bridge—a mini saga	132
Excerpts from lost novels	133
Living, growing	137
The bench	138
I saw your eyes today	140

About the Author	143
By L.A. Davenport	145

PREFACE

When I conceived the idea of writing a blog based around short stories, poems, mini sagas and drawings, I was initially stumped. Not only did I have no idea what I would call it, but I wasn't really sure what I would put on it. After all, it's all very well thinking a literary blog is good in theory, but it is another to put that theory into practice.

I realised I needed a concept, a sort of fictional framework perhaps, into which all the pieces would fit, so they would make sense as part of a larger whole. And as soon as I realised that, it occurred to me that my blog had to be a shop. Even better, It had to be the sort of magical, Victorian, anything-could-happen shop visited by the characters in the cartoons I avidly watched as a child. And seeing as I had been living in and writing about London for the last 12 years, it only seemed natural that this magical shop would be located there. But whereabouts in London? It is a big place, full of history stretching back centuries, and each area has its own special character that would have a huge impact on the type of shop, and blog, I created.

And then it dawned on me. Of course. The East End. The

one place left in London where vast swathes of ancient streets and buildings have been left almost untouched; where a magical shop could be allowed to to decay gently in the age of racing technological advances, to be discovered by pure chance by the writer, and reader, in need of inspiration. And what what would this fictional shop in the East End sell? Easy. Musical instruments.

That left only one decision. What should this magical shop, the one where all of my stories would be composed, be called? Now, that was obvious…

LAD, February 2012.

INTRODUCTION

In a lost corner of London, just outside the East End, lies a faded bow-fronted shop. No-one ever visits, but if you were to push open the creaking door and step over the piles of unwanted mail, you would find, in the dust-laden darkness, row upon row of shelves stuffed with trumpets, tubas, cornets, trombones, clarinets, drums. Each time one of the instruments is played, it tells a story, a different story every time.

This is the Marching Band Emporium.

NOTE

All of the pieces and drawings in this book were created and placed on *The Marching Band Emporium* blog during 2008 on the dates shown. In compiling this book, I have edited some of the written pieces, either to correct mistakes or to make essential improvements. Otherwise, they remain exactly as they were when I created them.

EXCERPTS FROM LOST NOVELS

[18 MARCH, 2008]

You see, I adore the applause. That's what keeps me going, really. That and the very experience of being on stage. The lights, the feel of the boards beneath my feet, the smell. You know, theatres have such a distinct smell. Something about the very particular mix of wood, varnish and plaster, I suspect, and the dust rising from the lights…

Of course, these places have lost a lot of their character. In the old days, when Gielguid, Ralph and dear, dear Larry trod the boards, it was all so different. Those were real actors. They made the very room come alive when they took the stage. As they emerged from the wings, you could feel a hush descend and all eyes turned to them. I tell you, it was as if the world didn't exist, except in them. Sometimes, one can almost feel their ghosts, urging you to give everything you have, to touch the audience with the unique magic of the theatre, as they so often did. It reminds me of when I was playing Horatio to Gielguid's Hamlet in, where was it? Guildford, I think. '55. Must have been. As I listened to him intone those marvellous words – Alas, poor Yorick! I knew him, Horatio; a fellow of infinite jest, of most excellent fancy... – I was transported, I tell you. I wasn't on the stage anymore. I was in a Danish graveyard, and nothing existed but Gielguid, that skull and me. Little me, so young and so naïve, really, rapt and learning at the knee of a master. A fellow of infinite jest. Indeed he was. And of most excellent fancy. Everyone adored him, you know.

Malcolm gazed at the young woman sitting opposite him in his tiny, faded dressing room, the light bulbs reflecting in her glasses. She shifted nervously in her chair and smiled weakly. Oh, look at me, Malcolm said. Here I am whittering on about my marvellous memories of the stage. You don't want to listen to all that. No, it's very interesting, the young woman said hurriedly. You are too kind, my dear. Too, too kind. But what have you come to talk to me about, snaring me in my private lair, my refuge? I love these moments, you know, in the hours before the curtain call. Everything seems so quiet, so peaceful in here, while the stagehands and theatre staff flit about outside my door, getting it all ready for my appearance. All that for me. So kind of them. So kind.

Well, Mr Bains. Do call me Malcolm, the old actor said, patting the young woman on the knee. Well, Malcolm, the woman said, smiling nervously. Your agent, David, asked me to come up to Oxford to see you this afternoon. Yes, my dear? He asked me to come up and talk to you about the show. Unfortunately, he, he has been detained in London, so can't come up himself...

That's very kind of David to send you...Angela. Yes, Angela, thank you. It is a shame that he couldn't make it himself, after all the years we have been working together, but I am charmed to have you here, Angela. Malcolm patted Angela on the knee again, smiling indulgently and leaning forward slightly.

The thing is, Malcolm, David is a little worried. About the show. The show, my dear? I must confess that my last couple of performances have perhaps been a little flat. I have been struggling with a slight infection and I know I haven't been able to give my anecdotes about the marvellous actors I have worked with over the years their normal zest. It may have explained some of the muted responses of the audience, but I shall soon be back to my best, having them rolling in the aisles and wiping tears from their cheeks, as I have done so many times in the past. Malcolm raised his right index finger and smiled triumphantly.

It's nothing to do with your performances, Malcolm. They have been fine. Great, in fact. Indeed? What is it? Do tell. Well, the thing is… Yes? The things is, sales have been very poor. The theatres we have done so far have been half full at best and we are struggling to sell tickets. We have tried everything. Campaigns in the local press, leaflets, posters, but the response has been…disappointing. Unfortunately, Malcolm…Mr Bains…Sorry, Mr Bains. Unfortunately, we can't sustain any more losses on the tour, and we are going to have to cancel the remaining dates. Including tonight? Yes.

Malcolm, suddenly crumpled, looked at his wire-frame glasses, folded neatly on the dressing table, and his make-up box. He hadn't started putting it on yet. No need for that now. He gazed down at his jacket and smoothed out a fold, feeling the rough tweed under his palm. I am old, Malcolm said, still looking at the material of his jacket. Is that what you are telling me? Too old? No, not all. Just…What? Unpopular? No-one wants to hear my stories anymore, is that it? I'm sorry, Mr Bains.

I don't have anything else, you know. I'm so sorry. What am I going to do? Malcolm looked up at Angela, tears welling up in his eyes. I'm all alone. I have no-one. The stage is my only friend. I have nothing else. I'm really sorry. Please. Stop saying that. Angela looked down at the threadbare carpet as Malcolm smoothed his jacket again. Shall I get you a taxi back to your hotel? Yes please, he said quietly. David told me to make sure that you got back to London okay. Did he? How very kind. He really should…Can I have a few moments to myself? I'll join you upstairs shortly, but I would be alone for a little while. Yes, of course.

TOGETHER

[30 OCTOBER, 2008]

You are on the sofa.
I am sitting further back
in the silent the room.

Your hair is curled
and your fingers hover
over the white plastic keys.

I watch you,
though I should be working;
the screen before me glows, unused.

You don't know I am watching you,
but you will turn,
slowly moving.

As our eyes catch, you will smile
And so will I
to be alone with you.

ANOTHER LIVING ROOM

[29 SEPTEMBER, 2008]

DREAM

[14 OCTOBER, 2008]

Do you dream? I mean dream the dream. You know the one. The one where you are a hot shot. Walking into a room, everyone turning their heads, nodding in appreciation and jealous recognition. Ah yes, the dream of the winner. How about the one with the sun on your smiling face as you drive along a California coast road in an open-top sports car? Is the wind ruffling up your hair, or haven't you got that far? That would mean you actually pictured you, your real self, in the dream. Maybe you aren't so convinced.

You need to be convinced. Believe, in a true way. What's the point, after all, in dreaming if you aren't going to actually see yourself driving in that car, walking into that room? That room, by the way. I think it is a champagne reception. You aren't the guest of honour, that is the artist who painted the incredibly "now" pictures on the walls that sell for thousands and made the sculptures in the middle of the room, the ones so cleverly lit from beneath. No, you are the person everyone wanted to come. The one who turns a gathering into an event. Yes, you.

But do you really believe it? That it could happen? If not,

it's just idling to imagine the scene. Just the channelling of brain waves into conjuring an episode, using memories culled from films you have seen and adverts you thought you hadn't taken in. On that California coast road, for example, are you driving in a vintage car or something rather new? Is there a song playing on the stereo? What is it? Is there someone in the passenger seat? Is it someone you know, or maybe a model or actor? Are you driving to impress or to enjoy? My, my, you could end up revealing so much about yourself. Those dreams, they are your hopes and your aspirations, but you have been taught them, you do realise that, don't you?

And that car. Do you really think you will be driving along a California coast road, sun-baked like the grey tarmac sticking momentarily to the hot rubber of your tyres? You don't even live in America, do you? No good thinking that someone like you will end up in that particular scenario. A boy like you, in a provincial town on the margins of hope? Forget it. You don't have the teeth for that glinting smile. Or the hair for the ruffling wind, come to think of it. Did you consider that you are a nobody? A mere trace on the retina of life? Your life counts for nothing. And yet you think you will end up on that coast road, in that vintage car, with the chrome trim and leather seats. Dream on.

EXCERPTS FROM LOST NOVELS

[12 FEBRUARY, 2008]

JIM SLOWLY CLIMBED THE STAIRS, PULLING HIMSELF UP EACH step by the handrail and wheezing slightly as he struggled to carry his tool bag. Finally reaching the fourth floor, he looked out at the tower blocks and railways of south London from the walkway and cursed the out-of-order lift. Eventually, once he had gathered his breath, he made his way to number 48, pausing slightly before pressing the buzzer.

Inside the flat, the old man woke with a start. The television flickered in the corner of the dirty, shabby living room and the cat circled in the middle of the floor, hoping his master would remember it was dinner time. The old man felt his forehead, wiping the beads of sweat into a shiny slime and shuddering as he remembered the nightmare that had tormented his sleep for the past week. The buzzer squawked once more. So that was it. Someone at the door. Who on earth could that be?

The old man shouted that he was on his way and tried to tidy up the hall as he approached the front door, throwing a pile of newspapers and an old, threadbare jumper through the open door of the bedroom. There was a thick, flat shadow on the frosted glass. It must be a man, he thought, and a tall, fat one at that.

Hello, I'm Drain Control, the overweight, middle-aged, balding man said with no sense of anything in his voice. The old man turned away from the door and walked into the kitchen. Not much of a welcome, Jim thought, following the cardigan-clad, bent back around the corner and into a dingy kitchen with stains on the walls and old, filthy saucepans on the hob.

Who did you say you are, the old man asked in a low voice. You called our office this morning. I'm Jim. Drain Control. The old man looked startled. What, he asked, with a wild look in his eyes. Drain Control, Jim said in a louder voice. The old man turned away and reached down to a draw, pulling it open with a fluidity that belied his advanced years. Slice or stab? Slice. The old man grabbed a bread knife and spun around, thrusting the blade towards Jim in a threatening manner. No-one is going to control my drains, he shouted.

Okay, okay. Fine, Jim said, instinctively raising his hands and backing out of the kitchen. If you don't want me to help, that's fine. The old man stepped forwards. I don't want your sort here, he yelled. Get out of my flat. Think you can come here and control my drains? You've got another think coming.

Jim grabbed his bag, which he had left by the door, and almost tripped over the door frame as he stepped out on to the walkway. As he retreated back towards the stairs, he could see the old man standing in the doorway, waving the bread knife and a light shining in his eyes.

They are never going to believe this back at the office, Jim, back in his van and staring at the dashboard, and the old man, back in his chair and gazing at the patch of carpet and the circulating cat, thought at the precisely the same moment. But I don't go to an office, the old man thought, checking his brow again before falling asleep.

SHATTERED—A MINI SAGA

[26 JANUARY, 2008]

I SOMETIMES IMAGINE YOUR LAST MOMENT—A DEATH-TOUCH of tearing metal and glass in the early evening.

While you sank away from me, I was struggling with a recipe.

When the ambulance arrived, I was laying out the plates.

As I began to think you had forgotten, the telephone rang.

DRINK, DRINK UP, MY FRIENDS

[6 MARCH, 2008]

THROUGH THE HOT-FUELLED EXCESS OF A LONDON SATURDAY night comes the rising call: Drink, drink up, my friends. Tonight we shall be drowned. The bitter acid taste of a glowing glass, drained to foster complicity. The swirling smear of a wooden room, a hand placed on your shoulder. You lurch your head around, blinded by the brassy bar and the smile so close to yours. There is a duty to perform, you have to be my friend tonight. Wait, you shall be back, there is another calling. You clamber up the stairs, fighting with your unruly limbs and blocking voices in your head. A bawdy conversation with someone you do not know, your hand steady on cold tiles. You must wash your hands, but spill water all around. A leering glance at the ladies' queue, imagining naked flesh. Don't trip on the stairs, my friend, everyone is watching. The coldness in your cheeks, the sweat upon your brow. You are a prince tonight, your mighty mind shall fly. Check your zip as you reach your table, throw a sloppy grin all round. There is another glass waiting, eager eyes are on you. Time to cut a dash, employ a little bravado. Glug down your pint, even though you know it is too much.

The liquid spilled upon your shirt, but no-one will ever notice. Your new-found friend does not remember you, locked in conversation. So what? You can steal some time with someone new. Up comes another rising call: one more to save our souls. Drink on, drink on. A syncopated shout goes up, others raise a hand and cheer. You look round at other tables, feel sorry for the tourist family. But there is no way out, you cannot cheat your new-found will. You stare at your yellow pint, watching bubbles slowly rising. Your hands have turned to lead, your eyes are becoming heavy. That hand upon your shoulder, a different willing smile. Drink it down, my friend, show me you are one of us. I will never part from you, as long as I shall live. Open your throat just one more time, it will all soon be over. You are the last to finish, something of a failure. They are parading out to smoke, suddenly it seems so tempting. The slamming rush into your head, it could go either way. What's that? They won't let someone back in, we are angry now and have to leave. Out on the cold street, you sway and almost fall. Look back at the bouncers, they'll regret not seeing your worth. Now time for that cigarette, it feels like nothing when you draw. An instant headache and cold limbs, but you must smoke on. Where to now, my perfect friends forever? You cannot stop drinking now, or the hole will open up. You fall off the curb, trying to test your balance. Half of them have already gone, they were never one of us. Shall we try that club? You have to face reality, the magic has upped and gone. A journey on the hated bus, all jerking nausea. The stumbling walk back home, the blacked-out echoing. Climb the stairs with broken legs, pulling with your hands. Walk past the bathroom door, you mum would not approve. You crave the tempting solace of your silken bed, the oblivion of sleep. But your mind circles in the street-lit room, there is no rest tonight.

DANCER

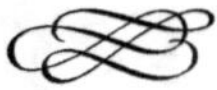

[28 JANUARY, 2008]

EXCERPTS FROM LOST NOVELS

[26 FEBRUARY, 2008]

THE WHITE VAN APPROACHED THE TURNING SLOWLY, DROPPING off the tarmac road and onto the long, ridged dirt track that led across an empty, ploughed field. Avoiding the water-filled troughs and holes, the van tentatively rolled along the track, steadily approaching a straggly copse that partially obliterated the outline of a cottage.

Soon, it was far enough along that drivers passing by on the road didn't even notice it, and its progress was so slow that the seagulls that had been swooping and squawking over the furrowed ground in the hunt for winter food went back their task and ignored it completely. Even before the van reached the copse, it had disappeared from all eyes and thoughts.

As soon as it entered the partial covering afforded by the leafless trees, the van slid to a halt on the muddy ground and a man in his mid-thirties, dressed in corduroy trousers, waxed jacket, checked shirt and wellingtons, opened the driver's door, which swung with a creaking jerk, and jumped out. He placed his hands on his hips and looked around, apparently deciding what to do next. Aside from the seagulls and the faintest sense of a breeze through the tangle branches of the trees, there was complete silence and nothing seemed to move. Moisture hung heavily in the air, and the entire copse smelt faintly of fungus.

The cottage, which was obviously abandoned and run-down, stood uneasily in a small clearing in the trees, threatening to collapse at any moment. The window frames were blackened and rotting, and there were missing panes of glass. The front door hung awkwardly on its hinges and the bricks were chipped and crumbling. In many places, the mortar was missing to such an extent that it was obvious that the wind, and rain, entered without hindrance. The dark, damp red bricks of the cottage's walls contrasted with the green-brown of the earth and the trees, and the distant grey of the sky, yet it seemed as if it had been there forever. He couldn't have hoped for anything better.

After a few moments of contemplation, the man turned towards the van and motioned to a bored-looking girl no more than eighteen years of age sitting inside. She reluctantly pulled her muddy trainers off the dashboard and, adjusting her vest top and bra, opened the door and stepped hesitantly onto the ground, pulling up her loose combat trousers to stop them getting dirty. Her pale, freckled skin developed goose-bumps almost instantly in the cold air and she was thankful for her long brown hair, which covered her bare shoulders. With a look of utter disgust on her face, she stared at the man.

What the hell are we doing here, she asked with loathing in her voice. I told you, he said we could find it here, the man replied. You have got to be joking, she exclaimed. I can't believe you dragged me all this way just to see this dump. And I'm cold, she added, looking at the ground. I told you to bring a coat, the man said, absent-mindedly, his attention drawn by a half-open window on the upper floor of the cottage. You aren't my Dad, you know, the girl replied. What are you looking at, she demanded. What? Oh, nothing. Come on, let's go inside. We might be able to light a fire or something, the man said, marching towards the front door. Yeah, right, the girl muttered to herself as she picked her way across the mud, avoiding the puddles.

Inside the cottage, the man purposefully strode around the ground floor, opening all the doors and checking the rooms. The last room he tried seemed about right. It had obviously once been a sitting room, with a moth-eaten sofa, open fireplace, peeling sideboard, shelves scattered with cheap ornaments and a battered valve radio. The large bay window looked out at the van and had a clear view of the dirt track. Perfect, he thought. It might be a bit cold, but who cares? She won't be complaining for long. He smiled to himself as he stepped back out into the hall.

She was standing by the front door shivering slightly, her arms wrapped around her chest. You aren't going to get warm if you leave the door open, the man said cheerily, walking back towards the kitchen but still watching the girl. As she looked up to give him a dirty stare, she saw a fleeting shadow and something swinging towards the man's head. Look out, she shouted.

He had time only to frown and think about turning round before he was struck heavily on the back of the head. He landed awkwardly on the floor, blood already seeping onto the worn rug. The girl looked at the man, horrified and frozen to the spot, suddenly alone.

From the kitchen, another man stepped out, much taller and thicker set and dressed in T-shirt and jeans. He was looking at his victim and carrying a table leg in his hand. Slowly, he lifted his head and gave the girl a piercing stare. Don't hurt me, she whispered, pulling her arms tighter around her body.

AN ARTISTIC DEATH—A MINI SAGA

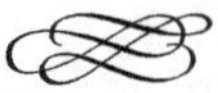

[18 JANUARY, 2008]

AN ARTIST LEARNED HE WAS DYING, AND SAW THAT HIS DEATH could achieve longed-for immortality.

He painted his decay and sculpted his suffering, revelling in his new-found inspiration.

But the strength he drew weakened those who loved him. And when he died, it was they who were cold.

THE INTERVIEW

[3 APRIL, 2008]

DAVID WATCHED THE HEADLIGHTS OF THE TRAIN REFLECTING off the tunnel walls and streaming along the silver ribbons leading out of the darkness. Although it was past rush-hour, the platform filled as the rattling rumble of the Victoria Line train become louder. David remembered a piece in the paper about a man who was pushed in front of an oncoming Tube train by a schizophrenic. He looked round at the faces of the swelling crowd by his shoulder. What does a schizophrenic look like? Anyone. He braced himself against a push in the small of the back and hoped the driver was paying attention.

The train stood at the platform for an age. No-one said anything. Just shifting feet and the rustle of adjusted clothes. A small cough and the turning pages of a free paper. And nothing. Just waiting. The electric motors powered down and suddenly there was the rumble of another train to another place on a platform that seemed miles away. The echo of another tannoy and footsteps. Must be a man in business shoes. The speed and pitch of the notes gave it away. Don't look at anyone. They'll think you are a freak. Touched

20

in the head. David could feel beads of sweat forming at his hairline. Too many clothes. You always get it wrong, you stupid idiot. When are you ever going to remember the Tube is hot, Central London is hot, racing through the crowds is hot? David dare not look at his watch. The interview was in half an hour. Easy if the train moves in the next five minutes. Should he jump out and walk? Someone ran towards the train but slowed as he saw the empty despondency in the passenger's faces.

The train jittered into life. Sorry for the delay, ladies and gentlemen. Apparently there was a problem with the doors on the train in front of us. But we are on our way now. Mind the closing doors.

Regent Street seemed wrong. Where were all the people? Of course, a weekday. Mid-morning. No-one to shop. All earning money to pay off the interest on their credit cards. David tried to walk slowly but inadvertently quickened his step as he thought about what he would say. What would he say? God knows. He hadn't had an interview for a job like before. He knew a little about the company, and a little more about himself. The idea that winging it makes it seem more natural, is that right? Couldn't it also make you look more, well, idiotic, unprofessional, unprepared?

The door pushed unevenly after he spoke to the voice on the intercom. Come up to the second floor. Thanks. Click, already gone and the door buzzing. Fine. He climbed two steps at a time and pushed open the glass door. How can I help you? I am here for an interview. David checked the clock above her head. Two minutes early. That's good. We don't have any interviews today. He froze. You're a day early. Oh, I see. The bottom fell out of his stomach and his heart shrivelled away.

David pushed open the uneven door and stood looking at

the pavement. He didn't know what to think. It all seemed so pointless. Always a failure. Always a failure. Eventually, he looked up. The city lay before him, glowing light and gold in the coming sun. Regent Street curving down towards endless opportunities. Tower blocks and palaces. It's all there. He took a step forward and smiled.

SOMETIMES

[24 JANUARY, 2008]

SOMETIMES, IT IS EASY TO SPEAK. THE WORDS JUST FALL OUT and you don't even have to think about the way you move your lips or the processes involved in forming the sounds in your mouth and throat. But just imagine if your mouth was glued together. Not literally, of course, but frozen, clamped together by…what? Fear, embarrassment, disgust?

It can happen. One day, long ago or far off into the future, I don't know, I found myself talking to a friend. We were, to all intents and purposes, walking down a busy street. It seemed like daylight, as I recall, but it could have been that the street lights and reflected glory of the capitalist saviours that line our shopping streets have given me that impression. It could have been midnight. Although, you would have thought I would have been tired, or drunk, and I don't remember being either.

No matter. Details are, by their very definition, tethers for the spirit. So, my friend and I, we walked and talked, observing other people on the street, and then forgetting them as our linguistic flights of fancy struggled to get into the air and then arced into the gutter, describing a parabola of empty digressions and pointless assertions. At some point, while thinking of what to say next, I traced one of these curves, and that was when I saw it.

A pigeon. I don't have an aversion to pigeons, you must understand. They are fine birds, in their natural habitat. Our particular brand of urban slime does not suit them, however, and, gripped at the throat, I stared in horror-filled fascination at a bird, hobbling around on a pair of stumps (his talons being missing) and his scrawny body showing through greasy, unkempt feathers that stuck out in clumps like the branches of a Christmas tree at the end of the festive season.

Not a pretty sight. One of his (why I am ascribing a gender to this ambling pile of litter is an interesting question in itself) eyes was covered by a puss-filled scab, which only served to enhance the impression of an animal on the edge of existence. Death would, surely, have been preferable, even to an animal that has not been programmed to think beyond his survival instinct.

I don't know why I was so entranced, as one can see such unpleasantness on almost any busy city street, except that I realised I felt more sorry for the bird than I did for the homeless man who sat in a nearby doorway, slumped over a cardboard sign. I suppose the argument runs that the bird is a victim of our nature-tampling activities and would not, ordinarily, live in such a concrete wasteland, whereas the homeless man does have choices. Lots of them. So, it is reasoned, he does not deserve our sympathy to the same degree.

However. The pigeon doesn't actually have to live in the city. It (he, whatever) could fly away to a wooded glade in an archetypal pastoral scene. But it takes the decision to stay on balance, based on a genetic algorithm handed down from generation to generation. The thing is, although the chances of being maimed by traffic and contracting horrible diseases are high in an urban sprawl, natural predators, which it is, after all, primarily programmed to avoid, are less common. And it is easier to hide from those that are there in the endless brown-grey cliffs. There is also the fact to consider that, in the city, food is more plentiful, even during winter, when it is less cold than in our pastoral scene.

The homeless man, on the other hand, could be on the edge of psychiatric illness, an alcoholic, a victim of crime or a property crash. Perhaps he is divorced and the subsequent emotional and financial strain left him without a house and without a job. Once out of the system, it is almost impossible to get back in, as it is entirely geared to ushering in the new and the young, not the deadbeats with broken spirits and gnarled skin. It could be that he is stuck, more of sinned against than sinning, and cannot break free.

So I turned those thoughts over in my mind, while my friend continued to talk about nothing at all as if it was everything that had ever been, and concluded that everything is not what it seems. Sometimes.

CURLED UP

[21 APRIL, 2008]

EXCERPTS FROM LOST NOVELS

[1 APRIL, 2008]

THERE WAS NO EXPLOSION. NO TRACE OF A SOUND. NO-ONE heard anything, or so they said. But something must have happened. After all, there it was, in the middle of the road: a crater the size of, what?, a large tent? A small car? Who cares. What is more important is that, right outside the Co-op on Caledonian Road, there was hole in the tarmac so big that the road had to be cut off for several hours until it was known whether or not the whole thing would collapse, taking the shops and houses with it.

Of course, the gas people blamed the Piccadilly Line, which runs beneath the street. Engineers from the Underground said it must be a burst water main, and the water people said it was probably caused by the men from the cable TV company, who had been digging up that part of the road only the week before. The police didn't care who's fault it was, as long as someone did something about it. So they leaned on the local council to get it fixed, who ran around in circles until Irene from the Road and Highway Maintenance department had the bright idea of shoving responsibility onto Transport for London. But they pointed out that Caledonian Road isn't a Red Route and so technically not their problem. Irene went off sick with work-related stress for six months when that e-mail came in.

For those of us living along the street, it was a fairly large patch of excitement that occupied us for several days. Fantasies and conspiracy theories floated up into the air like empty crisp packets, twisting and turning until they drifted into a dark corner and were forgotten about, to be swept away in the cold light of day. I'd like to say that I didn't believe any of them, but I didn't not believe them, if you see what I mean. After all, there wasn't much else going on.

On the day when the hole was discovered, the life of the street had been pretty much as it had always been. It was a summer's day and a hot, dry wind forced pollution and dust into everyone's eyes, and conversations, such as they were in the endless roar of traffic, concerned either the weather or the upcoming England match. And then, at around 4pm, and with no warning, the hole appeared. It's a good job the driver of the number 91 bus was watching where he was going. As it was, he almost drove straight into it. The passengers tutted to be thrown around by him slamming on the brakes, but they didn't mind once they knew what he had done. He received a bit of adulation in the end, with a photo and a write-up in the local paper. Humble Hero Saves Locals From Bus Plunge. Apparently, he was a married father-of-four, but that is beside the point.

What is strange is that there wasn't any rubble. No sign of a collapse. Nothing but a clear tear in the ground, showing the layers of tarmac and cobbles, and the clay earth beneath. It seemed as if a giant mouth had come down and bitten a chunk right out of the road. Of course, no-one seriously put forward that idea, but there wasn't any better explanation. And when the hole was filled in, and the cables and pipes had been repaired, there was no more talk of theories, and the smooth road had only a dark stain to show that anything unusual had ever happened.

But something unusual had occurred, as we discovered when another hole, of almost identical proportions, appeared further up Caledonian Road towards the railway bridge, with its old advert for Pirelli tyres faded under the relentless onslaught of the weather and exhaust fumes. There was no bus this time, but the hole was there all the same. And that was when I got involved. It didn't happen just like that, you must understand, as I had, like everyone else, gone back to my humdrum, some would say almost boring, life. But I was inexorably drawn in, dragged into a series of events that I am still trying, after all these months, to understand.

MORNING

[20 MAY, 2008]

Morning breaks steadily over the brickscape. Tepid
light seeps around railway arches, warehouses, factories,
drawing a thousand million lines along decaying walls,
picking out the edges of grime-smeared broken windows
and a thousand million cracks. Ghosts shuffle in the growing
light, scraping across the crumbling tarmac, worn down to
dust. The growing roar of traffic mingles with the strains of
distant, fading… A shout and a breaking bottle. Stumbling
steps and hoarse, empty laughter.

The ghosts, no more than shadows, with grey skin and
open mouths, sway from side to side along the narrow pavement, remembering life, remembering what they might have
been. The green trees shine. Too bright. Too alive. The
houses, across the wide grey canyon, too upright, too reso-
lute. A hateful reminder. Birdsong pierces disintegrated
minds, lacerating souls. The world is a prison, the ghosts its
inmates. Keep to the shadows.

A thousand million miles away is comfort, protection,
respite. Even redemption. An insurmountable distance lies
ahead. An insurmountable obstacle. The ghosts cannot be

seen, cannot be touched. They must hide, away from the others, away from voices, eyes. So they huddle together, ignoring the reproachful stares, the hissed slurs. They know already. They know they are ghosts, no more than shadows. Twisted mouths and blasted eyes, pulled down, down into the netherworld.

The tepid lights seeps on, growing, filling, pushing into the dark corners. And the ghosts slowly vanish, shuffling to safety, escaping into a parallel reality, not to be seen until the light fades once more. The noise of the world rises, waves crashing over the brickscape, tearing at its decaying walls and grime-smeared broken windows. Lost among the railway arches, warehouses, factories, a ghost lies, alone, forgotten. The sun breaks through the clouds, illuminating grey skin and blasted eyes, piercing the soul within, crumbling the shadow to dust.

SOCRATES IN THE DUST

[19 JUNE, 2008]

Socrates Giannakopoulos stopped and looked down at the ground by his feet. While the old women in black cardigans, with their arms weighed down by bags stuffed full from the market, pushed past and the children waking home from school stared, Socrates stood motionless, contemplating the red, sliver and gold object lying the dust by the door of Mr Antoniadis' house. Where could it have come from? The thought of what the object might be did not cross his mind. All he could think about was how it got there.

After a few moments, during which Socrates tilted his head and stepped around the curious object in order to get a better view, almost stepping into the path of a cyclist racing down the narrow cobbled lane as he did so, he crouched down on his haunches, slowly pushing out his hand until it was just a few millimetres away from the red surface. The object was strange. There were two cubes, one small, one big, attached to each other. The larger of the two cubes had two, well, sticks coming out of its sides, which ended in small hooks, as well as two bigger sticks that pointed downwards in parallel and ended in stumps. On the small cube, there were two small silver squares painted on towards the top, with a small silver dot in the middle and then a silver line, edged in gold, along the bottom. On the larger cube, there was gold and silver lettering in a language that Socrates could not read. What was it made out of? It definitely wasn't metal or wood. Must be something Socrates had never come across before. Oh, and there was a small metal spike sticking out of one side of the big cube, with a small white cog on the end.

What have you got there, Socrates? The small boy jumped, falling into the wall of Mr Antoniadis' house and hurting his shoulder slightly. Er, nothing. Socrates didn't look up, sensing the shadow of authority above his head, and scrambled to hide the curious object. However, before he could do so, a large hand had already gathered it up. Socrates cursed himself for not having taken the object home straight away. But his brother would have snatched it off him and broken it.

So, Socrates, where did this come from? The boy turned to face the shadow. It was Mr Seitaridis, the science master from his brother's school. I…I don't know Mr Teacher, sir. I found it just here. I was wondering where it had come from. I thought it might have fallen from heaven. Socrates pointed up into the sky. Mr Seitaridis laughed, much to Socrates' dismay. Well, it might have fallen from the sky, young lad, but I am not sure it came from as high up as you think.

Mr Seitaridis examined the object for a moment while Socrates jealously stared at the red, silver and gold flashing in the teacher's huge fingers. Do you know what it is? No, Mr Teacher, sir. I was just about to pick it up and find out. Mr Seitaridis bent down onto his haunches and placed the object upright on its two long sticks. Can you see that? The boy followed the line of the teacher's finger towards the small cube, now at the top. Yes. That, my boy, is it's face. Suddenly the two squares became eyes, the dot a nose and the silver and gold line a mouth. And can you see that? The finger pointed to the strange lettering on the front of the big cube. Yes. Well, that says Super Robot. Do you know a robot is, Socrates? No, Mr Teacher, sir. The young boy was almost breathless with anticipation. It is a mechanical man that can move all by himself. The boy looked into Mr Seitaridis face with wonderment. Really? And then he fell sad. But it isn't doing anything. It doesn't move at all. Mr Seitaridis smiled. Just you see.

The teacher picked up the robot into his hands once more and turned the small white cog. Click, click, click. On and on he turned, until the robot stopped clicking. Carefully holding the legs still, Mr Seitaridis placed the robot onto the cobbles. As he let go, it picked up first one leg and then another, slowly moving forward, leaving traces in the dust by Mr Antoniadis' front door. Eventually, the robot fell over as it stepped over a large cobblestone, but the boy was transfixed. What do you think, Socrates? It's amazing, Mr Teacher, sir. You take that home and play with it, my lad, and next time I see you, I might show you how it comes alive. Mind you don't turn the cog too much, or...

But Socrates wasn't listening any more. My brother will be so jealous, he thought. I can take it home and show him, and Mum. And I'll tell Dad when I speak to him in my prayers. I have a Super Robot that comes alive. The boy looked up at Mr Seitaridis and thanked him. The teacher smiled in reply and waved Socrates goodbye, leaving him sitting in the dust by the door of Mr Antoniadis' house, cradling his red, silver and gold object.

JUST A JOKE

[9 APRIL, 2008]

SILENCE. OKAY, THERE WAS A SMALL, STIFLED COUGH, AND maybe the creaking of someone shifting in their chair, but the auditorium was, essentially, silent. A mass of people, all staring at me with a mixture of boredom, pity and, in several cases, pure loathing. From where I stood, it seemed as if I had maybe 10 seconds at most before someone would tell me to get off. And then, I was sure, everyone would start booing and shouting.

What could I do? I couldn't very well tell a joke. That was what had got me into this mess in the first place. Telling jokes. Whose idea was that? Well, mine, as it happened. Entertain them, Andy had said. Just a couple of minutes between the acts. You know, the usual thing, just so we have enough time to clear the stage and get the props and gear on for the next lot.

The usual thing. I didn't notice those words at the time, as I was caught up in the excitement of being involved in what could be loosely described as a cultural festival. Andy had been walking through his office, talking as he went, leaving

35

me trailing in his wake, trying to keep up with his fast pace while appearing enthusiastic. Suddenly, we were by the reception and he had stuck out his hand. Thanks, I am really pleased you are on-board. We have got some great acts, really innovative and challenging, and entertaining, of course. I think you will fit right in. I shook his firm, warm, confident hand, my head spinning slightly. I managed a shaky smile. Great, see you in a couple of weeks.

The usual thing. Easy to say, and easy to think you know exactly what is required. But, when I sat down to think about it in the pub the night before the festival, it occurred to me that I was in a far bigger mess than I had realised. What would there be in the theatre? 3000, 4000 people? I had no idea, but I knew it would be a lot. I saw some stand-up performing there a few years ago and I was impressed that he could hold that many people in the palm of his hand, turning them this way and that before finally releasing them, warm, happy, lifted, into the cold night air. What on earth was I going to do? Okay, I didn't need to hold forth on a range of topics and be consistently funny for an hour. Just five two-minute segments to keep an already excited audience pepped up before the next lot came on. They wouldn't be there to see me, just kill time without getting bored. For the vast majority of them, I would be completely unknown. What had I done? Written a book on modern culture and made a couple of appearances on late-night TV programmes on obscure digital channels. Hardly what people would call setting the world alight. I only got the job because I happened to know Andy through a friend. Of course, that would make it all the more embarrassing if I screwed up…

Just before I stepped out in front of the closed curtains and faced the audience, I didn't feel nervous. Perhaps a little delirious, but not nervous. I hadn't had a drink, just a sneaky fag round the back of the theatre. This will be okay, I thought to myself. The first act—an African drum troupe – had gone down well, and with good reason. The audience were clapping wildly and the performers were delighted, if a little relieved, as they poured past me and the stagehands got to work on changing the set. 3-2-1, go. I stepped out onto the small strip of stage in front of the curtain and looked around. Lots of people. Lots. Dry throat, sweaty palms. Where were the comforts of the TV studio now, with their retakes and glasses of water? And no audience.

My mind went blank. The applause was still dying down, so it didn't matter too much. And then it popped into my head. A joke. Something by a risqué comedian, probably that one I saw a few years ago. So, I breathed in and gave it my best. It didn't occur to me until the second after I finished… Inside, I was shouting: I am not a racist. Or a homophobe. Nowhere near. Okay, the accent wasn't a great idea… But it was far too late to explain. Four thousand people hated me in an instant. I looked towards the wings. Andy stood with his head in his hands. I could feel the disappointment seeping out of him. There was an assistant signalling 30 more seconds. I turned back to the crowd and laughed nervously.

I don't know what came over me, but I started to be honest. I explained that I was nervous and that I was nobody, not really. I promised I wouldn't attempt anything like this again, once the evening was over. But I wouldn't let Andy down, so they could expect me again after the second act. Without any jokes. I made another nervous laugh. No-one reacted. The room stayed silent. I didn't care. I was just relieved that they hadn't started booing and shouting for me to get off. So, in a louder voice, I announced the next act, the name of which had miraculously popped into my head a second earlier, and turned to walk off. Silence. My footsteps echoed as I walked the narrow strip of stage. And then a small ripple of applause started to reverberate around the auditorium as the curtain was raised on the next act. As I walked past Andy, he just stared at me. Hatred, disbelief, anger? Actually, all three.

VIEW OF PLACE DES ARCADES, ANTIBES, FRANCE

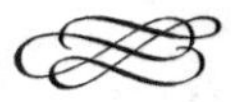

[25 AUGUST, 2008]

EXCERPTS FROM LOST NOVELS

[15 MAY, 2008]

I THINK I'LL JUST HAVE A SIT, IF YOU DON'T MIND. IT'S BEEN A long day. Michael said nothing. He carried on looking out over the empty sea front and the waning tides towards the darkening horizon, his hand resting on the back of the concrete bench. That's better. Why don't you sit down and join me. No, thanks. I'd prefer to stand. Don't be silly. I can't talk to you properly if I can't see your face, and I can't be turning round all the time. No good for my hips. The doctor said I shouldn't put too much pressure on them. Not in my condition. Come on, have a sit. A swollen, red, cracked hand patted the weather-beaten concrete. We can talk proper, then. Do we have to talk?

Just the soft breaking of tired waves and squawking gulls seeking pickings from the discarded fish and chip papers. A family walking back to their car, dragging tired children and plastic buckets. The strains of holiday music blaring out from family restaurants and neon bars. And the soft wheezing of the old man, his swollen, red, cracked hand still lying where he had patted the bench. A chill whipped through the air and an empty plastic bag rolled along the tarmac causeway. The sand turned to grey as the anaemic sun dipped slowly below the edge of the world, lending the grey, billowing clouds scudding across the sky a purple-red glow. In a disjointed flicker, the yellow-blue-red lights strung along the sea front stuttered into life, revealing broken bulbs at irregular intervals.

The old man stared at the horizon. Used to be a nice place, this. In the old days. Michael clenched his hand on the rough concrete, anticipating the boredom of another story he had heard a thousand times before. Oh yes, it was a right old place, full of life. Everyone from round about, not to mention those that'd come by train. They all came here in their time off, when factories'd be shut down. Never mind your Benidorm and your Costa del Sol, or whatever they're called. In them days, this was where it was all happening. He pointed a swollen, red finger at the concrete. A car horn sounded somewhere behind them and a bus trundled past.

Used to bring you here when you were a nipper. Don't suppose you remember that. Michael cleared his throat. Yes, I remember. I thought it was the best place ever. Seemed, well, colourful. He looked up and down the sea front and thought of the bland fish meal they ate for lunch and the shabby restaurant, with its cheap furniture, dirty tiles, stained cutlery and bored, sloppy waitress. He tried to match his childhood memories of endless sunshine, sweet ice cream and hours spent building sandcastles to what they had seen that day. He cleared his throat again. Can't imagine that now. Can't imagine any kid finding this place...exciting. It's just a dump. The old man shifted slightly on the concrete bench. Aye, well, times change. There's much that doesn't seemed to have retained it's former glory. Why don't you sit down here. He patted the concrete again.

Michael looked around. He felt stupid standing behind the bench, even though there was hardly anyone to see, and maybe he would be warmer sitting. But that would be giving in. Mind you, he couldn't imagine going back to that horrible bed and breakfast and still not be talking. God, what a horrible place. Those bed clothes must be infested. They have to be. And the fusty Victorian chintz. No, the worst must be the tiny bedside lamps. All that dust. Did they ever clean the place?

He looked up and down the sea front again and walked slowly around the back of the bench, running his hand along the concrete. Sitting down, he placed his palms flat on the rough surface by his sides. The sun was almost gone now and the sea slowly darkened. There was no beach any more. No sea front. No yellow-blue-red lights. No shabby restaurant. No bed and breakfast. After a few moments, he sighed. I'm sorry. The old man wheezed. I know. He felt a swollen, red, cracked hand alight on his and wanted to cry.

THE RUSH OF LIFE—A MINI SAGA

[9 JULY, 2008]

A MAN LAY WATCHING AS GLISTENING LARVAE BURROWED DEEP into his belly.

He grew weak and his belly slowly filled, twitching with the insect cargo forming within.

After interminable months, a thousand dragonflies burst out, filling the room with the rush of clicking, flapping wings.

He never felt more alive.

TEST YOUR INTELLIGENCE!

[14 MAY, 2008]

IT'S 8:30 IN THE EVENING. YOU ARE IN YOUR LOCAL BAR having a few drinks with some friends after a tough day at the mine head. Out of the blue, one of your group, a man you have known for a while but to whom you haven't really paid that much attention, says something that makes you think for a moment. Not only that, but all the girls in your group start flirting with him and a passing barmaid even slips him her telephone number, purely on the strength of him making that statement. Wow, saying that sort of thing makes him seem really clever, you say to yourself. I wonder if I am as clever as him?

Now you can find out! With our special questionnaire, developed in conjunction with the British Academy of British Academies, you can measure your intelligence from the comfort of your own home. Yes, that's right! Just answer the 10 questions below and check your total score against our intelligence profiles at the end of the quiz. It's that simple! Good luck!

1. To what degree does a dog derive pleasure from food relative to that experienced by a human? *Yes/no*
2. Discuss the different uses of the term "crack" using words of exactly eight syllables.
3. Taj Mahal. More/less/about the same
4. If fashion is art and art is fashion, where does that leave the Ford Focus? 1 2 3 4 5 6 7 (Circle most appropriate answer, where 1 equals candle wick and 7 equals lightbulb, where candle wick represents starry, starry night and lightbulb represents due-laden morning)
5. If a man comes up to you on the street, do you feel. Yes/no
6. Panic buying is the new spelling. Fine/suspended sentence/prison term
7. Utter three banalities on the role of Nursultan Abishuly Nazarbayev in the Gap business model.
8. I told you I didn't mean it. Yes/no/about the same
9. Fill an envelope with yoghurt and place it in the freezer. Remove after three hours. Do you see: The face of God/the face of a dog/a black shoelace?
10. If you knew I was watching you while you were filling in this questionnaire, would you still have completed it? Yes/more/7

SO, HOW DID YOU DO?

- 64-65. Fantasy mind games. You are very intelligent, but are likely to struggle when discussing the finer points of Hegelian philosophy.

- Q, R or S. Lipstick mirrorball. You are quite intelligent, but Brutalist architecture leaves you cold.
- >. Dappled sunlight. What did your mother tell you? Pay more attention at school and you will go far.
- 1. Dogtooth check. I told you not to believe everything you read. It seems easy to say now, of course, when the evidence is placed before you, but any old fool could have guessed that. Put down the spray can and the statuette of Pope John Paul II eating a glacé cherry and go outside. You will feel much better.

EXCERPTS FROM LOST NOVELS

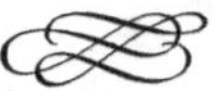

[15 APRIL, 2008]

BEN LIFTED HIS EYES AND SQUINTED AT THE OCEAN-BLUE SKY. Sunlight baked the hard, unyielding grass and ancient carved stone. Ripples rose from the ground, swimming the nearby trees and pomegranate shrubs in a sea of relentless heat. The guide was still talking but Ben couldn't be bothered to listen any more. Temple…Greek…Doric columns…open-air altar…decorated frieze…Hera…550 BC… The air ricocheted with the clicking and sawing of insects and Ben could hear his heartbeat pounding in his ears. The material of his shirt was hot and he could feel dampness in the folds around his armpits. He remembered the shop by the entrance and wished he had bought a bottle of water.

The guide, wearing a cap with a piece of material over his neck, started to move away, and the other members of the group, struggling in the heat and walking slowly, followed, the grass crunching beneath their feet. As the guide's voice became lost in the rising air, Ben lifted himself from the steps of the temple, wiping the pale dust from his hands and inspecting the red indentations left by the sharp stones. Have you been to Italy before? Ben jumped slightly and felt a headache instantly rise through his skull. He stared at a woman standing just a few feet away. He wasn't sure whether he had seen her before, but there was something... Er, yes. Are you on the tour? No, I am in the shop. Her accent was soft, almost not Italian. She pointed towards the entrance with a lazy arc of her arm. I go for walks when it is quiet. It's very quiet today.

Ben looked at her again, noticing her soft dark curls loosely tied up and dark, large eyes. She placed her hands on her hips and smiled. Shorts. She was wearing shorts. Tanned, long legs and canvas trainers. And a striped t-shirt. Not pretty. Graceful. Glowing. Almost majestic. Ben couldn't seem to take her in. He had spent the whole morning turning down his brain to primary sensations. Sharp, soft. Hot, cold. Bright, dark. The breath rose hot from his lungs and he sighed. Do you like Paestum? Yes. Very nice. It's a bit warm. But the temples... He swung his arm around, looking at the ancient building again. No, for the first time. The temples are beautiful. He smiled and squinted as he looked back at her. Did you see the painted tombs? The... she frowned and looked away... tuffatore? What is the English? Yes. Diver. Did you see that? Yes. He looked so real. Made me want to jump in the sea. Ben's mouth was dry and his throat hurt as he tried to swallow.

You want to swim? Ben frowned. It would be cooler. You are uncomfortable in the heat? He felt embarrassed and tried to hide the growing damp patch under his arms. We are used to it here. She paused and gazed towards the rippling trees. I love the quiet. Ben listened to the insects and...nothing. He looked over at the receding tour group. He could vaguely pick out the guide's flat drone through the rising air and the clicking sawing, and felt a little guilty. They would be finished soon, and he didn't want to appear ungrateful. Where would we swim? In the sea. It's close. Over there. She smiled and pointed over the trees. Do you want to come? But, the tour… How would… Don't worry, I drive you back to your hotel.

Ben looked at the ancient stones, but already felt cool saltwater on his skin. He smiled. I don't know your name. They call me Maria. And you are Ben. She thrust out her hand, slim and tanned, with long, plain nails. His face fell involuntarily as he took her hand, so cool and calm in his. Something, a sensation, flowed through his hand. How do you… How do you know my name? She smiled conspiratorially and held onto his hand. I've been waiting for you. For a long time. He stared into her eyes, unable to pull away.

Come, let's swim. As she turned and pulled him gently towards the trees, he looked back at the disappearing group and felt in a daze. He couldn't remember, couldn't think. Just the heat of the sun and the cool of the coming sea. He tried to focus on her shorts and tanned legs, her strong back and slim arm reaching back to him, her fingers entwined in his, unbreakably bound to him, glowing through his hand. A branch hit him in the face, the leaves sharp on his skin. He closed his eyes and had a flashback to the hotel, the square outside. The market, the beach. The shaded branches by the restaurant. Her. Her face, everywhere, in every crowd…He opened his eyes and stared, his heart pounding… Come, or the tide will go out.

FORT CARRE, ANTIBES, FRANCE

[26 AUGUST, 2008]

THE CANCER WITHIN

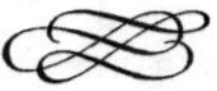

PART I

[15 JULY, 2008]

WATCH YOUR STEP. THE TALL, WELL-BUILT MAN IN THE BLUE
cap stooped as he gently nudged the small girl into the lift.
He looked up and smiled at the girl's mother, who was
already waiting inside. Such a pretty child. What's her name?
Poppy. The tall man looked back down at the girl. Hello
Poppy. Mind your back, little one, the doors are about to
close. The girl, in a pink dress and with her hair in pigtails,
stared up at the man. She looked worried, but turned away
coyly after a few seconds of contemplating his steady, warm,
unthreatening smile.

Everybody in? The man looked around the large lift,
quickly recounting the members of his party. Fifteen. The
usual crowd, he thought. All in their regulation outfits and
with their Wellness badges clearly displayed. Good.

Doors closing, he called out in a cheery voice. The large
metal doors slid silently into place and, with a slight jolt, the
lift descended, the numbers on the counter by the tall man's
head slowly ticking by. UG, G, BG, B, -1, -2, -3… As you can
see, ladies and gentlemen, and little girls… the tall man
smiled at the girl, still coy and wrapped around her mother's

legs… we are descending right into the bowels of the earth. From the visitor centre, which is just above ground level, we will go down several hundred feet, to the -15th floor. As you are doubtless aware, the Wellness Correction Centre is located in an abandoned mine, from which our ancestors used to dig up coal to burn for heat, energy and light. There are even a few of their abandoned tools and drills in a special exhibition area of the visitor centre.

A few of the passengers sniggered. The man smiled indulgently at the more incredulous passengers. It does seem strange now, but there was a time when there was doubt as to whether nuclear power could satisfy all of our energy requirements. It was even suggested that we would ruin the planet if we carried on with what they saw as a polluting technology. More sniggers.

However, we have got past such banal concerns now. After all, what does a country such as Britain need with wildlife when we all live in cities. Ah, here we are.

The lift doors opened and the passengers stepped out in to a large, white room with a reception desk at the far end. Aside from the two large, air-tight doors flanking the reception desk and a piece of multicoloured Computerised Academy art on the left-hand wall, the room was empty. No chairs, nothing on the walls. Just bare reinforced plastic. The tall man waited until everyone had left the lift before following and walking over to the reception desk.

Hello Sandra. I've got the next party for you. Are you ready, or should we wait a few minutes? My talk took a little less time than usual this morning. Sandra smiled at Adam and looked down at a screen by her side. Looks like the party before you are still in there. They are nearly done, though, so it will only be a couple of minutes.

The tall man tapped the top of the reception desk with his index finger and turned to his party, who were regarding the

Computerised Academy art. Lovely, isn't it? He spoke to no-one in particular. One of the people who had sniggered earlier turned to the tall man. How do they get it to have such rich colours? Well, as you know, all the colours in the artwork have been chosen based on scientific principles in order to help guide your mood to it's optimum state for this specific environment. The questioner nodded enthusiastically.

As we are in a Wellness Correction Centre, the Magna 5 computer that produces these artworks on behalf of the Wellness Department examined data on the ideal state of mind for a person visiting such a centre, given what they are about to see, and the sort of mood that we would like them to have when they leave. Matching this data to a predetermined colour and pattern palette, the task then became one of the computer creating the most evocative and stimulating work that would achieve the required mood set. Finally, the piece was sent to one of our factories, where it was etched into plastic and mounted. As you can see… the man swept his arm in front of the artwork… the quality of the finish is second to none. The group nodded and sighed in appreciation, and the mother lifted up the small girl so that she could see better.

Ready for you now, Adam. The tall man turned and smiled at Sandra. Great. He ushered the group towards the left-hand side door, which slowly swung open with a hiss. Once through, Adam walked over to a large metallic hoop and pressed a button on the nearby console. Sorry, folks. I know you have been scanned already, but we just like to make sure before you enter the Wellness Correction Gallery. You would be amazed, but we still get people in who want to do something stupid.

The group laughed and chatted happily among themselves as they stepped through the hoop in single file. As each person passed, a sensor raced along a track inside the hoop, projecting a high-intensity ultrasound beam through their body. In addition, a sensor read the code on their Wellness badge, matching it up to a DNA sample taken when they arrived at the visitor centre. As the small girl went through the hoop, her mother guiding by the shoulder, an alarm rang out. The rest of the group turned and stared disapprovingly at the mother. Adam stepped over and knelt down by the girl. She was scared and shaking slightly. Don't worry, Poppy, he said in a soft voice. I think it must be this. He reached over and touched a small, shiny butterfly clip in her hair. Slowly withdrawing the clip he stood up and went back to his console. Try again. The mother pulled Poppy back by the shoulder and gently pushed her through again. The alarm remained silent and the group went back to talking among themselves. The mother passed through the scanner and Adam smiled as he handed the clip to her. The scanner upstairs must have missed it. Not to worry. The mother, relieved, took the clip and pushed it into her hip pocket before patting her daughter on her head.

PART II

[17 JULY, 2008]

ONCE ALL THE PARTY HAD PASSED THROUGH THE SCANNER, Adam led them along a narrow, white passageway lined with more Computerised Academy art, each successive picture subtly altering the party's mood until they had entered a state of passive acceptance. Only the small girl, who had been concentrating on Adam's confident, unhurried walk, remained nervous. She slipped her hand into her mother's, absent-mindedly squeezing the long fingers and picking at the tastefully manicured fingernails. But there was no response. Even when the girl stared at her mother and tried to speak, her mother's face remained blank and empty, staring straight ahead as she walked in a steady, even step. After a few moments, during which the entire party was silent, they reached another door, this time made of bare metal and with a small reinforced glass window towards the top. Adam stepped over and entered a code into a small keypad at elbow height. The corridor was instantly filled with the sound of whirring and a series of clicks before the door slowly withdrew into the wall. Adam turned to the group, smiling as he ushered them over the raised threshold.

The other side of the door, the party was greeted by a long, wide corridor, at either end of which stood heavily armed guards in helmets and body armour. The floor, ceiling and one of the walls were made of metal, while the remaining wall consisted entirely of reinforced glass. Towards the centre of the glass stood a small pedestal, adorned only with a single, large red button. The group moved slowly along the corridor, first looking at the guards, who stared back at them impassively, and then turning to look through the glass, until they had almost filled the space. All the while, several cameras traced their every move.

Through the glass, the visitors could see that they were standing in a gallery overlooking what appeared at first glance to be a giant laboratory. Dozens of workers dressed in Wellness Department uniforms and carrying computerised notepads silently moved between large machines with flashing panels and banks of screens set into the walls, all the while taking notes and making alterations to the settings. Towards the front of the laboratory and behind an opaque screen that separated them from the workers, twenty cushioned metal chairs were arranged in a semicircle. Into each of the chairs, a human being had been strapped at the wrists, feet and head. Wires ran from gaps in their identical white jumpsuits and into the backs of the chairs, and tubes had been inserted into their mouths and nasal cavities. From the gallery, it appeared that they were peacefully asleep, with the slight trace of a smile on their lips. However, their eyes were hidden by metal discs, with yet more wires running out the discs and into the back of the chairs.

Adam slowly walked over to the pedestal and cleared his throat before he turned to the party, each member of which fixed their gaze on him as he began to speak.

Welcome to the Wellness Correction Gallery, ladies and gentlemen. I imagine that most of you know what it is that you are seeing and why you are here. However, it is also likely that not all of you are aware of the full range of work that we do at the Centre and its importance in maintaining the stability and prosperity of our country.

He paused and looked at each of the faces staring back at him, hanging on his every word. Only the small girl was not concentrating, and she began to fidget as he continued.

Perhaps you have been aware of some of the important events that have occurred in recent weeks from the downloads that you have received in your FutureSafe News chip.

A few among the party nodded seriously.

It is certain that we, as a people and as a nation, stand on the brink of greatness, of finally achieving all that our forefathers could possibly have dreamt for us. It is also equally certain that, at such times of overwhelming importance, it is crucial that each one of us, as individuals and citizens, do all we can to ensure that the plans our wise and benevolent leaders have devised for us are realised as fully as possible.

Adam looked around the room, quickly glancing at the guards before he continued.

Yet, amazing as this might seem, it is apparent that not everyone in the country is willing to make the small effort required to help us, help everyone, in our united quest.

He turned towards the glass and looked down into the laboratory. As he spoke again, his voice dropped almost to a whisper.

These people, ladies and gentlemen, these people are either unwilling or unable to make that small effort.

As Adam said these words, the small girl became curious and let go of her mother's hand. She slowly pushed in between the legs of the people standing in front of her, picking her way through the group until she was next to the glass. She placed her palms on the cold surface and looked around the room below, gazing at the machines, the workers in regulation uniforms and the people strapped to the chairs. Turning back towards the party, Adam lifted an index finger and jabbed the air.

Those plans, to turn us once again into the greatest nation on earth and deliver a peaceful and fulfilling life to every citizen, those plans, which each and every one of us endorsed when we signed the Declaration of Unending Support, mean we cannot waste valuable resources on people who are not willing to dedicate themselves unselfishly and wholeheartedly to the nation. Such people, ladies and gentlemen, such people need to be…corrected. Permanently.

As Adam finished speaking, the corridor was filled with an ear-piercing scream that made the party of visitors jump. The guards instantly snapped off the safety catch on their weapons and placed a finger over their personal alert buttons. Everyone turned towards the source of noise. The small girl was leaning with her back against the glass, a look of abject horror on her face. She stared at her mother, whose passive expression began to crumble at her daughter's anguish, and pointed towards one of the chairs in the laboratory below.

It's Daddy. Daddy's down there.

FINAL PART

[28 JULY, 2008]

ADAM QUICKLY SCANNED THE OTHERS MEMBERS OF THE PARTY, trying to read their faces. His mind raced as he contemplated having to abandon the visit. No, everyone was still passive, if a little agitated. Glancing at the mother, he could see that she was struggling to maintain her composure. Adam gritted his teeth slightly.

Why do we still bother with giving birth in the traditional way, he thought. It only causes problems with attachment and empathy. How can such feelings be anything other than enemies of progress? The sooner we can create people in a laboratory without the need for wombs or invent some drug that stops mothers loving their children the better. All empathy does is ruin people, makes them useless to the state.

As he looked away from her in disgust, he realised that the guards were staring at him, and he shook his head slightly. Even through their helmets, which covered their entire faces in opaque protective plastic, he could see them relax. Slowly, they re-engaged the safety catches on their weapons and lowered the muzzles. Adam became aware of the slight whirring of the cameras as they tracked and recorded the reactions of everyone in the room. He stiffened. Sandra will have pressed the alarm. They will be watching. All of them. I"d better get this right. They really won't accept another party having to be permanently corrected. They might even correct me. He sighed. Why did they even think this visitor centre would be a good thing? I know it plays well on the FutureSafe News, but can't they just create images from the databank? It would be so much easier.

As the seconds ticked by, the members of the party slowly pacified their minds and started to breathe normally again. Only the mother maintained her grief-stricken expression. Adam glanced at her and then at one of the guards. He flicked his head and the guard nodded slowly.

Adam turned towards the little girl. Tears were streaming down her face and her eyes were darting from person to person. As soon as she looked at Adam, he smiled, slowly, gently. Daddy is down there, she wailed. Mummy. The girl shouted and tried to run to her mother, but Adam stepped forward and swept her up before she could escape, balancing her on his arm and staring into her face. She was so small and light. I want my mummy. She wailed again. The girl's face was contorted in pain and wet. Her cheeks and eyes were red.

Poppy. Adam spoke gently as he continued to stare into the girl's eyes. Poppy, do you know what is happening here? He stroked the girl's back with his thumb as he balanced her on his arm. The rest of the party watched them intensely. The girl sniffed and nodded her head slightly. She whispered into Adam's face. Daddy is going to be corrected.

Yes, that's right. But do you know why?

The girl shook her head and started to cry again, quietly this time. They turned towards the glass and looked down into the room below. A guard stepped forward and, firmly taking hold of her elbow, quietly led the girl's mother away.

No-one in the party paid any attention. All eyes were fixed on Adam. The far door of the room closed with a soft click and the guard returned to his post.

Can you point to your daddy? The girl raised an arm and extended her index finger towards a chair in the middle of the semicircle.

He's there.

Adam adjusted his arm slightly. He looks peaceful, doesn't he.

She nodded.

He is peaceful, Poppy. He is practically asleep. He hardly knows where he is. Maybe he thinks he is back in your little flat in City 5, or even in the home he lived in as a child. Who knows, but you can be sure of one thing. He isn't suffering.

The girl wiped her face and swallowed. Adam looked into her eyes.

The important thing for you to realise, Poppy, is that we never correct anyone unless we absolutely have to. Do you remember the lessons you learned in your Dutiful Citizen classes? The girl nodded slowly. Do you remember why we have to correct people sometimes?

Yes.

I am sure your teacher has told you, and your Learning Chip has reminded you, that every person has to sign a pledge that they will live a healthy and moral life, and that they will do all they can to support, maintain and further society. After all, our futures are reliant on that. Every single one of our futures. Do you remember that Poppy?

Yes.

Well, your daddy signed that pledge too. But I am afraid to say that he broke it.

You know, people are corrected for all sorts of reasons. Mostly, they are correct for engaging in undesirable habits, such as smoking, drinking, eating unhealthy foods, not getting enough sleep, not doing the regulation amount of exercise, for being overweight, for doing activities that carry risks, for not wearing regulation clothes, for not wearing breathing masks while out on the street, and even for having sex with an unauthorised person.

Adam paused.

Poppy, when someone does something undesirable for Ultimate Wellness, they are putting themselves at risk of being unwell. That means they will need to have treatment in order to become well again, to be kept alive and productive, and that puts a strain on our resources. As a nation, as a society, we cannot have people wilfully putting their wellness at risk. It's like a cancer within, and it has to be cut out.

Adam readjusted his arm and glanced around the room. The guards were standing in the corners, relaxed, the muzzles of their weapons lowered. Everyone in the party was concentrating on what Adam was saying and the woman was gone. He looked up at the cameras. I hope they like this upstairs, he thought, before continuing.

Many centuries ago, it was felt that, when people became ill, they should be kept alive at all cost, regardless of whether or not they had brought it on themselves. They believed in the sanctity of human life above all else. However, it was quickly realised that doing that required so much money that it was threatening the development of the nation. The... selfishness of people not trying to be well was harming us all.

Poppy was staring down into the laboratory, more with curiosity than alarm. She watched the slow, steady breathing of the people strapped into the chairs. Although she found it hard to follow what Adam was saying, it felt familiar. It made sense. It felt right.

Of course, we didn't start correcting people straight away. We encouraged people to change their behaviour. We gave them advice, spelled out the risks, gave them the choice.

While some people made the right decisions and started to live better lives, many didn't, and it was obvious that we had to encourage them a little more. And that was the beginning of Wellness Correction. We took tentative steps at first, withdrawing treatment for those who did not protect their wellness and refusing them jobs, but it was when we realised that there is no such thing as the sanctity of human life when that life is not helping society as a whole that we made the real breakthrough. It became obvious that Wellness Correction was not just important on a practical level but was also a moral imperative. How could it be anything else?

Adam paused. Poppy shrugged her shoulders slightly. Her head was beginning to swim. How could it be, she thought.

Of course, we do much more than correct people at the Wellness Department. We genetically test every embryo before it is inserted into their mother, with all but those with an acceptable genetic profile discarded. We permanently correct all infants born with defects and those with below-desirable learning abilities or physical capabilities.

We continually monitor children as they grow, and all those with suspect tendencies and those who are not developing optimally for their assigned life task are also corrected, sometimes permanently.

And the rest, all the rest, are given the opportunity to live as perfect a life as possible. All those vaccinations and wellness pills, and the constant check-ups, they are designed to give us optimal wellness and help us reach our maximum productivity. So it seems almost criminal that someone who has made it to adulthood should reject all our help and not look after themselves. Wouldn't you agree Poppy?

The girl nodded. He face had dried now and her cheeks and eyes were no longer red. Adam glanced around again. Everyone concentrating, passive. Good. Turning back to Poppy, he continued.

Your daddy is here because he won't pursue wellness. The girl looked up from the laboratory and into Adam's eyes.

Do you want to know what he did that was so bad?

Yes.

He started to drink alcohol, Poppy. Why would he do that?

The girl shrugged her shoulders again.

After all, we have already created heart health pills that contain the nutrients found in red wine that lower blood pressure and reduce cholesterol. What possible purpose could there be in drinking? All it does is fog the brain and reduce productivity. It increases the risk of disease and it makes people change the way they think. They forget about their pledges and their unending support and they become unreliable. We can't have that, Poppy. How can your daddy contribute maximally to the furtherance of our society when he is doing that to his body? We paid for his education and his health as he grew. We, all of us, own his body and his life.

At first, we tried to be lenient. His morning breath scanner detected traces of ethanol and he was picked up on the way to work by a Wellness Department operative. He underwent the usual correction procedures, and pledged never to drink again. That lasted for a few months, but he soon slipped back into consuming alcohol. We found the people he was getting it from and had them permanently corrected, but your daddy was a persistent offender.

It troubled us all to see him break his pledge, it really did, so we bent the rules and corrected him a second time. But there is only so much we can do, Poppy. Your daddy is ruining it all for everyone with his drinking, as are all the people in the chairs down there, who have done a whole range of things to damage their wellness.

They are going to destroy all that we want for our futures, your future Poppy. We cannot let them do that. And it wouldn't be fair on them to let them keep on with their lives the way they are. They cannot be happy being so unproductive and disruptive.

Poppy shook her head.

So, seeing as all our efforts have failed, we have a duty to help them, and us. We really don't have any choice. It really is for the best.

Adam stepped towards the small pedestal, adjusting his arm so that the girl was comfortable.

Poppy, all we need to do to is to press that red button. Can you see the button?

Yes.

Would you like to press it?

The girl reached out a delicate, slim finger towards the large red disc, her ponytails falling in front of her face as she leaned forward. She caressed the smooth plastic surface, and felt it sink slowly beneath her finger.

AFTER HEARING YET ANOTHER DISCUSSION OF DANTE'S INFERNO

[23 OCTOBER, 2008]

Poor old Dante Alighieri.
He wrote the most divine of comedies,
charting a journey through heaven and hell
and all that lay in between.

He used his skills to settle old scores
in his Florentine world,
puncture the pompous
and lend wings to our rusty morals.

But, for all his lofty aims
and his gossamer-winged paradise,
we wallow in the mire of Inferno
and never look beyond.

Poor old Dante Alighieri.
His name carries down the ages,
but he could never have guessed,
it's the smut that sells.

EXCERPTS FROM LOST NOVELS

[22 APRIL, 2008]

Night falls slowly through the skylight, the stars shining pale through the blanket of pollution. The room is dark, illuminated intermittently by silent images flashing on a television screen. A man lies deep in a sofa, his feet outstretched on the painted concrete floor, listening to the distant roar of the city, waiting for something, nothing, anything.

Eventually, he pulls himself out of the enveloping material, stretching slightly as he reaches his full height. He brushes down his dark shirt, turns off the television and walks over to the door, pulling on a jacket and picking up his keys, heavy in his hand. Deliberately, he empties his mind before reaching for the handle, pushing all thoughts, desires away. No decisions, just instinct. It's the only way.

Out in the dark-lit corridor, he strides quickly, counting the numbers on the doors as he passes. 505, 504, 503, 502, 501. At the lift, he stops, wondering whether to walk down, but pushes the button anyway. Far away, far below, an electronic recording of a bell chimes and greased cables pull the metal box along its runners, whirring with mechanical efficiency.

The street echoes to his footsteps. A drunken couple cling into each other, a lone taxi, a distant empty bus. Hooded buildings folded into orange shadows and bricks melted into blacked-out windows. The takeaways are almost empty. Drawn faces tidy up menus, talk quickly on mobile phones, shave meat from rotating spits, the gas grills glowing red in the neon glare. Was that a fox? A thick, heavy tail disappears into the shadows.

Adverts shine in the centre of the roundabout, urging financial investment opportunities on the rats and sleepless birds. He considers walking straight across, the serried empty lanes useless at this hour, but turns down the ramp and enters the stinking subway. In the graffitied tunnel, he walks taller, watching the arguing couple, the fast-walking boy with waxed-down hair, the singing drunk. He runs his fingers across the metal lattice of the closed Tube station gates, thinking of the empty platform and the mice that run between the tracks. A pile of unwanted newspapers, an abandoned dustcart, blankets in a shop doorway, the acrid smell of old urine. The blankets move as he approaches. Spare any change, mate? A thick, dirty hand emerges and eyes, shining in a streaked and bearded face, stare. The man stops, still looking ahead, and pulls a wallet out of his jacket before stepping over. The fiver briefly connects them and the man is drawn into the shining eyes. God bless you. The hand disappears and the eyes fall away. Take care of yourself, the man says, before straightening up and walking on.

He feels the cold breeze on his face as he turns away from the roundabout and down a side road lined with Victorian terraced houses. Where is it? 105. No, must be the other side. He crosses, looking left and right, despite the lack of traffic. That's it. His stomach tightens and his breath shakes in his chest. Tingling in his fingers. You aren't supposed to be nervous. Maybe a quick cigarette. He fishes in his pockets and pulls out a pouch of tobacco and a packet of papers. He rolls badly and curses silently as the cylinder struggles to light. As he exhales, he notices a woman standing in an upstairs window, the light behind her head like a halo. Dammit. He walks around the next corner, stopping out of sight.

A car passes and a cat steps slowly, deliberately from behind a skip. He throws away the half-smoked cigarette and walks cautiously back into the street, pulling on a pair of leather gloves. The woman has gone and her window is dark. The key sticks slightly as he pushes it into the lock. But the door opens easily, and he steps into the dark hall, slowly letting the lock slide back into place. Silence. Almost oppressive. After a few seconds, his eyes adjust and he treads carefully over to the carpeted stairs. A board squeaks as he takes the first step and he stops, listening. Nothing.

At the top of the stairs, he pauses, looking at the three closed doors, grey in the half-light. No lights on. Not a sound. He flexes his fingers and rotates his shoulders. It would be so much easier with a gun or a knife. But they don't want it that way. After all, he will be unarmed, they said. The man breathes in and tenses his frame as he steps forward towards the middle door. Wait. What was that? It was in another room. A sigh? Silence. He relaxes and then tenses again, pulling his left shoulder back. With a crashing burst, he kicks the door open and flings himself into the room.

THE BOX

[30 APRIL, 2008]

Even in a sealed, empty box, there is constant movement.

Imagine a clear perspex cube, all the air sucked out before it was sealed, creating as perfect a vacuum as you can achieve under the circumstances. There appears to be nothing but the transparent plastic, bulging along the edges of the faces and at the vertices, where the methyl methacrylate resin pooled and gathered in the extremities of the mould.

Place your hand on the other side of the box and look through. Your fingers are fat and deformed by the two layers of plastic through which you see them. As you move your fingers, they flow, break, reform as if caught in a flash flood, water pouring over their surface, moulding the sandy flesh beneath. A pretty, or disturbing, effect, but the point is that you can see your fingers clearly, no matter how grotesque they appear. They are not obscured by anything.

In other words, you know there is nothing inside the cube. You can see that. It is, as the saying goes, self evident. To suggest otherwise would seem like madness. And you know that a vacuum, or as best as can be achieved, was created when the box was sealed. We have established that already. So, as you weigh the clear cube, as clear as your conscience, in your hand, you can be sure that, a few stray molecules of air aside, so tiny as to be irrelevant, there is nothing that could create movement inside the cube.

And yet.

There is a nagging problem. One I probably should have mentioned before now. The thing is, the walls of the solid, still, empty box you are holding are actually moving, vibrating.

At absolute zero, kindly revealed by William Thomson, 1st Baron Kelvin, in 1848 to be −273.15 Celsius, all the molecules within an object are still. Perfectly still. At that point, the object can justifiably be called solid. However, even a tiny increase above that temperature causes the molecules to vibrate and the slow journey to becoming a recognisable liquid begins. As the temperature rises further, the molecules vibrate more and more until they start to move around. The solid object melts. But nothing has changed, just the degree of movement.

So, you stand there, regarding your clear plastic box, apparently solid. Yet the molecules within the walls are constantly vibrating, full of potential, fizzing with…life? And as a shaft of sunlight breaks through the clouds and bursts into the room, the exposed side of the cube heats up. If the temperature were to increase sufficiently, the molecules would start to break free, assert themselves. They would flow.

I tried to turn my mind into an empty perspex box. Completely transparent. All thoughts sucked out before it was sealed, creating as perfect a vacuum as I could achieve under the circumstances. I thought I had accomplished something. I thought I had created perfect stillness, peace, even. But I didn't reckon on the fact that my mind was a liquid. The heat of the world was all around and I couldn't stop the vibration. I was fizzing with potential, with life, whether I liked it or not. And, as the temperature rose, my mind asserted itself. It flowed.

Only absolute zero would halt the flow, the constant movement, the endless vibration. Only then would I be at peace.

MARTY THE DAPPER WOLF

[21 JANUARY, 2008]

IS THIS LOVE?

[1 JULY, 2008]

SHE LIFTED THE BLIND AND LOOKED DOWN ON THE STREET below. Just the same trees and cracked pavements, stained yellow by the street lamps. There was no-one, and no sound, aside from the whirring of the air conditioning unit from the shop across the road and the distant wail of a siren. In the tower block opposite a darkened room was occasionally illuminated by an unseen television. Two floors above, an England flag hung, dirty and torn, from the bottom of a window.

Slowly she lowered the blind and turned back towards her room. She had almost forgotten the television playing in the corner and the man lolling on her bed. She watched him as he stared at the screen, adjusting his position and laughing at nothing at all. You've got to see this, babe. It's so funny. She looked at the screen, at the dancing colours, and listened to the jumble of noise from the tiny speakers. She smiled and laughed when the man did, but felt nothing.

The same posters on the wall, battered and torn at the edges. The same clothes pouring out of the wardrobe, and the same dressing table that she had sat at when she was a girl. The same hair, untidy and growing all the wrong ways. The same belly pushing through her vest top and the same thighs filling her tracksuit trousers. The same skin, and those ugly hands. She stared at the man lying on the bed. Come and watch this with me, babe. He patted the bed and smiled at her. She smiled back, nervously. What's wrong, babe? You don't seem yourself tonight. I can't relax. I feel all uptight. She frowned and placed her hands on her hips. You want me to roll you a joint? No, Mum would smell it. Anyway, you know I don't really like that stuff. Her face fell and she looked up at the cracked and stained ceiling tiles. Yeah, I guess.

Do you like me? She frowned again as she spoke. What? He glanced up at her before staring back at the television. Yeah, of course, babe. Seriously, do you like me? I said yes, didn't I? She sighed and looked at the television. I could turn it off, she thought. But what we do then? And Mum can't hear us with it on.

She smiled and jumped on the bed, landing on her knees. I've got an idea. What? He carried on staring at the television. Why don't we go out? Eh? Your Mum won't let you. We could say we are going to the shop up the road. 'Spose. Why do you want to do that? Dunno. I fancy being outside. It's really warm tonight, and we'd be out of this room. And we could, you know, talk. We talk all the time, babe. His voice trailed away as the noises from the television became louder, and then burst out laughing. You have got to see this, babe. It's so funny. She turned towards the screen. Nothing at all. Are you seriously watching that? It's rubbish. What? It's brilliant. She turned back to him and tried to look into his eyes. Come for a walk with me. In a minute, babe. It's finishing in a minute.

Outside, she tried to put her hand in his, but he pulled away and started gesticulating as he told a story about a friend who had been stopped by the police. Words flowed one after another but they meant nothing. All she could hear was the crunching of dust under her cheap flip-flops and the slapping of the soles against her heels. At the shop, she stood outside as he went in to buy a milk drink and a packet of cigarettes. An old man from the other estate was walking his dog on the other side of the road. He stared at her as she swung on the lamp post and ignored her smile.

As they arrived back at the flat, the man said he had to go home. She tried to look into his eyes but he stared at the floor. Won't you kiss me? The thought raced round and round her mind as she waited, leaning in slightly. But nothing happened and he said goodbye, glancing up and smiling. See you tomorrow, babe? Give me a call. We might be out at my Gran's. In the evening? Maybe, I don't know. He turned and walked away. The girl stood in the doorway by the entry phone, watching his lolling gait and wondering if this was love.

PRISONS

[10 JUNE, 2008]

ALL OUR LIVES, WE LIVE IN PRISONS, VOLUNTARILY, WILLINGLY, with open eyes and open arms. From the womb, we are trapped, entombed, yet we pull the edges closer around us, folding ourselves into the warmth, ensuring we never want to escape. Every institution we every enter and every home in which we live, they are prisons all. They close us down, but we desire that more than anything. And as we shut our eyes to sleep, we will safety, trusting we cannot be reached, hiding our wayward spirits in the darkness.

And yet.

Sometimes, we want to escape, to jump the fence and run, run toward the endless, limitless horizon, bursting out into the sunshine. We want be free. It tugs and drags at us, and we stare out into the emptiness, imagining the soft ground beneath our bare feet and the gentle breeze across our naked skin as we surrender ourselves to enticing unknown. We will live freely forever, we believe. And we will never look back. But can we ever escape? Can we ever live outside the prison walls?

Eventually, we realise we were born prisoners, and prisoners we shall remain.

EXCERPTS FROM LOST NOVELS

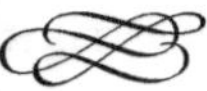

[26 JUNE, 2008]

THE WELL-DRESSED MAN SLOWLY PULLED ASIDE THE CURTAIN, feeling through the thick, heavy material the wooden rings sliding against the metal rail. Inside, the room was dark, and the smell of stale, damp air, mixed with human sweat, attacked his nose as he entered. It had taken him an hour to find the house in the forgotten back streets of the city, and the initial feeling of relief he had experienced at realising he had reached his destination soon was soon replaced with a dread sense of unease when he had knocked on the wooden door and it had swung open of its own accord. The house was silent, save a series of unearthly groans coming from the first floor, and he became aware of his footsteps as he walked slowly across the bare, dirty boards. Twice he called out before a small, thin voice from somewhere within the bowels of the house replied. There was no light, save for the patch of winter sunshine that illuminated the hallway from the open door, and it had taken him several minutes to realise where the voice had come from. He wasn't aware of how long he had waited in front of the filthy curtain before he had drawn it back, but now he stood, trying to adjust his eyes to the blackness and trying to revive the compulsion that had driven him to seek out this woman from another world.

Come in. The man started, but gathered his composure. The voice had come from somewhere over to his left, but he could still see only vague shapes. Don't worry, you won't fall. Let the curtain go and I will light a candle. The man did as he said and he heard a match strike, catching sight of a thin, bony hand in the yellow glow. The wick took several seconds to catch, during which the man wondered whether he should run away, back to the safety of his house, his life, but he stood firm, willing himself not to shiver. Once the candle had lit, he was able to see the face of an old woman sitting hunched in a threadbare armchair between a dirty stove and a small bed covered with a thick blanket. The woman was dressed in what appeared to be a pile of rags, and her greasy, straggly hair stuck out an angles from beneath an old bonnet. Aside from the bed and stove, the room was sparsely furnished, with just a single chair in the middle of the room and a battered trunk pushed into a corner. On the wall above the bed hung a smoke-stained picture of a street scene, while the wall opposite had been daubed with a series of strange markings drawn in what appeared to be brown ink, although it struck the man with a shudder that it could just as easily be blood.

Why don't you sit down? The woman motioned to the chair and the man perched himself on the edge of the seat, trying not to make his clothes dusty. You have come a long way to find me, particularly as you chose to walk all the way. Why didn't you bring your carriage? I didn't want anyone to know I was coming. I thought so. She nodded her head slowly. Is that because the idea made you feel uncomfortable, or because you didn't want to get your wife's hopes up in case I failed to help her…

How did you know? The woman waved her hand dismissively. I make it my business to know. You would be surprised what an old woman who never leaves her room can find out about a gentleman, especially an old woman with friends like mine. She laughed and shook her head. Yes, I can find out a lot, and you couldn't imagine what sort of clues law-abiding, morally upstanding people like you leave lying around about themselves. When you have nothing to hide, there's nothing you can hide, you know.

The man looked at the floor. After a pause, he looked back up at the old woman and frowned. So you know why I am here? Yes, after a fashion, but I would prefer if you told me yourself. The man looked around the room again and cleared his throat. Well, a few months ago, my wife became ill. Yes? Very ill, as a matter of fact. We took her to see several doctors, each of whom told us a different story. Hah, doctors! The man looked up at the woman and then slowly down at the floor. One said she had pleurisy, another consumption, another a derangement of her circulation, and yet another said she was merely hysterical. In each case, the doctor wrote out a prescription for ever-more expensive medications, none of which made her any better. As a matter of fact, most of them made her worse. One doctor even suggested blood letting, which made her so faint that I thought she might die. The old woman inclined her head. Very upsetting, I am sure. Yes, it was. My wife was distraught and I don't mind saying that I was at my wit's end. Indeed, the old woman said gently.

Eventually, I decided that enough was enough. I withdrew a substantial portion of my savings and took her to see the Queen's Physician. At first, he didn't want to see us, but an acquaintance of mine put in a good word for me and I secured an appointment with him. After a thorough examination of my wife and a lengthy consultation, he told me that my wife had a cancer of the lung resulting from an injury she had sustained when she had slipped on the ice last winter.

Not only that, but there was no treatment and she had only a few months to live. That was two months ago, and she is fading away day-by-day. The woman shifted slightly in her armchair. Terrible, terrible. The man fell silent, trying to gather his thoughts and fight back tears.

And now you have come to see me in the hope that I can in some way help your wife? The man lifted his head. Yes.

There are a few possibilities that come to mind, and you are certainly not the first gentleman I have had in my chamber asking for help in such matters. However, there are several considerations we must address before we get to that point. While I shan't cost you as dear as the Queen's Physician, I will incur certain…expenses. I understand. I am not without money. Good. The old woman frowned and pointed a finger at the man. And you must do exactly as I say, no matter how strange or outlandish it seems. You must understand that, without following my instructions to the letter, it will be impossible for me to help your wife, and she will die. The old woman's eyes seemed to glow in the half-light, trapping the man in their gaze.

Anything. I will do anything.

THE OTHER LUTHER

[19 NOVEMBER, 2008]

Six weeks ago, a small man in a large hat swept into my office. As he strode in and pulled off his wide-brimmed hat, his cape brushed the leaves of the pot-plant by the wall and, I noticed with a small degree of irritation, knocked a few sheets off the top of a pile of rejection letters received by the disappointed novelist who shares my working space twice a week. Just before the small man, who I later learned was called Ignatius Pugh, entered the room, I had finished reading a seed catalogue in preparation for a piece I am contracted to write about the hidden flower war of 1978 between Luxembourg and Kazakhstan, and was about to make myself a cup of tea. Consequently, I was ill-prepared for his dramatic entrance, which I greeted with complete silence.

You will forgive me for disturbing you. He spoke with utter confidence. I looked at the scattered rejection letters and frowned. I might, I said. How can I help you? The small man pulled a chair from the corner of the room, knocking over my briefcase and a picture of Doris Day I had been meaning to put up for weeks, and arranged himself dramatically in front of me. You have a power, Mr Edmundson. I do? I wondered how he knew my name but then spotted a sheet of my headed note paper on the expanse of empty desk between us. What power? The power, my friend, to be heard. Oh, I see. I sat back in my chair, a little disappointed. You want me to write an article and get it published in the papers. And you think that, because I am poor, I am unscrupulous and desperate and will write anything for a bit of cash and the chance of fame. The small man sat back with a broad smile on his face and clapped his hands. Precisely. He laughed. We understand each other so clearly, Mr Edmundson.

I can't say I wasn't a little disappointed at him making no attempt at flattery, but I soon overcame my scruples. It turned out that Mr Pugh expected me to believe that he was a time traveller, and that he had gone to see the brother of Martin Luther. I was too peeved that he should expect me to believe this to bother to check whether or not Martin Luther actually had a brother, so simply carried on taking notes.

Mr Pugh insisted that, at the same time as his more famous brother wrote the 95 Theses, in 1517, Johann Luther devised a set of ideas or creeds through which man may live with man peaceably. However, as the younger Luther brother believed that there was no place for God or religion as a guiding force in men's lives, his ideas were derided and he was ostracized by society, even by his own family. Mr Pugh then claimed that, having learned of the existence of Johann from a contemporary historical account, he had used his newly developed time machine to travel back to 1517 and take down his ideas first hand, so to speak. However, he had time only to note the first seven of Johann's tenets before Mr Pugh realised he had to come back to our present time for an important business meeting.

Of course, I didn't believe a word of it. For a start, I am

fully convinced that it is impossible to travel back in time. And it was obvious that Mr Pugh had never been to modern Germany, let alone the Germany of Luther and illuminated manuscripts. Also, it is impossible that Johann Luther would be familiar with the Buddhist-influenced concepts that the tenets espouse.

No, it was quite clear that Mr Pugh had wanted simply to dress his own rather woolly ideas in the cloak of respectability offered by association with the early Protestant movement. And it was apparent that he couldn't think of anything more to say after he got to seven notions.

But he paid well. So, as I watched him swish his cloak once more, knocking a standard lamp over in the process, and leave my humble office, I decided that he was harmless enough and his ideas were worthy of presentation. So, I leave it you, dear reader, to decide their merit:

- All men are equally valid
- All ideas should be judged as valid only in terms of their internal logic
- All actions should be judged as valid only in terms of their preceding intentions
- Religious belief or its lack does not, in itself, justify any action
- No man may assume authority over another without explicit consent
- There is no such thing as morality
- No thought is less or more valid than another

SHADOW OF ME

[26 MAY, 2008]

EVERY DAY—A MINI SAGA

[2 DECEMBER, 2008]

A FOX, STILL. A DOG, WATCHING. A LEAD QUIVERING IN MY hand.

Every day, the fox sits in redbrick gardens, a whiskered down-at-heel.

Every day, the dog strains, flattered by the timidity of raw nature.

Today, cold picks at our ears. The dog searches vainly. The sad lead falls slack.

MANHOLE

[8 DECEMBER, 2008]

HELLO. CAN YOU HELP ME? I SEEM TO HAVE GOT MYSELF stuck. Sorry to be a bore. I know you must be terribly busy, but if you could just spare a moment... No? Of course not, I understand. Maybe someone else might... Ah, yes, hello. No? Maybe he might... Hello? Sorry to bother you. Wouldn't normally... Hello? Yes? Sorry. It's all a bit embarrassing, I know, but I was wondering... No? Excuse me. Sir? No... Not at all. Don't worry. I realise this is a bit of an imposition. Hello? No? I'll be fine. I'll just wait here until someone... Funny, really. I mean, me ending up in this, well, manhole. Stuck, you know. A man, in a hole... Just in case anyone does fancy... I mean, if they have the time, as it were. Just a tug should do it. A quick pull on my hands. Wouldn't take a moment. Everyone is so busy this morning. Ow. No, sorry. My fault. Shouldn't be stuck down this hole, then you wouldn't end up having to kick me in the back on your way to work. Gosh, it is busy, isn't it. Lots of people... Ow. Yes, sorry, I know. Shouldn't have got so drunk. My fault for getting married, of course. The fellows, they had to do some-thing. Mark the occasion. Mind you, I think even they excelled themselves with this particular wheeze. What was that? No, madam, I am not mad. Just talking out loud to whoever will listen, as it were. Hoping to attract some attention, maybe convince someone to give me a hand. You know, a quick tug. No, I can assure you that it wasn't my intention to find myself stuck halfway down a manhole in the pavement right outside Victoria Station at 9:00 on a Monday morning. Yes, I realise that it is an inconvenience, but it was never my intention... No, no, just overweight, madam. I prefer overweight, if you don't mind. My feet aren't on anything, just dangling, thank you for asking. Rather an odd sensation, if I may say. Like floating, I imagine, although I have never been much of a swimmer... Ah, yes. Would you excuse me, madam? Good morning, kind sir, I could indeed do with a hand. Maybe a quick tug...No? Just fancied a laugh at my expense? I see. Well, who can blame you? I am sure I would have done the same. Ow... Yes, another kick in the back. Very sharp shoes you have there, sir. They could serve you well in some sort of combat situation. Ah, wonderful, a group of Japanese tourists. Just what I need. Do I mind? What? You taking your photograph with me? No, not at all. Go right ahead. I think you're going to have to crouch down, if we are both going to get in the picture... You want me to smile? Right. Well, there we go. What was that? A typical English ritual? I suppose so. In some ways. Is it traditional for a man who is getting married...? Yes, yes, that's right. Playing a trick on the groom. Very funny, unless you happen... No, I was hoping to get out before now. Ever since I woke up this morning to the sound of the pavements being cleaned at 5:00. No, no-one has helped me. Actually, pretty much everyone has ignored me. And there have been a few laughs at my expense, I can tell you. No, you were the first who wanted to take my picture... Is that a policeman? No, just over there, near the public telephones. Could you attract his attention? Got to get a taxi. Of course you have, but it wouldn't take a moment. You're in a hurry. Of course you are. And what is five more minutes to me, after all? Don't worry, he's spotted me. I can see him coming over now. Ah, good morning officer. How are you today? Yes, indeed, as you say. In better shape than me. I dare say. Well, to be honest, you are not going to believe what has happened to me…

THE STATION

[27 MAY, 2008]

THERE IS A STATION, NOT FAR FROM HERE. PLATFORMS arranged in lines, ribbons of metal running into forever. Metal tubes carrying tired faces far, far away. Bodies slumped in multicoloured seats. Laptops and books, papers neatly folded. Arms folded, eyes closed.

In the falling darkness, I am sometimes there, watching the metal tubes as they fill, feet running alongside, wheels clicking, urgent eyes searching for empty seats. A series of electronic beeps and it is all over. Doors sigh into place, motors whirr into life, pulling the tube along the ribbons, into forever.

All those people, they have lives. Beds, televisions, back-home kisses, keys lost in the sofa, bags dropped on hallway carpets. Quick shower and a meal. Open a packet and throw yourself down. Flick the channels and drag yourself to bed. The ironing can wait. Tomorrow is another day.

The faces always change, maybe the metal tubes too. But the station remains the same. Fast food, newspapers by the door, quick-fix remedies. Porters with dustcarts and charity workers looking for signatures. Buy a watch, kill some time. Stare at the big screen and catch some silent news.

On a muffled day, the sun a hazy blur, I found the station silent. No tubes, no clicking wheels, no tired faces. Just a glow of orange on a far-away man. A lazy pigeon swooping and a closed kiosk, its shutter chipped and bent. The tiled floor clean and gleaming, dotted with chewing gum black holes.

One day I went back to the station. Platforms arranged in lines, ribbons of metal...forever. Air filled with exhaust, burning acrid voices into my mind. Running feet, urgent eyes, electronic beeps. They were all there, perhaps as I remembered them. But the station was not the same, and neither was I.

EXCERPTS FROM LOST NOVELS

[3 JUNE, 2008]

A SMALL MAN WITH A ROUND CHEST STEPPED OUT OF A SIDE door at the back of the bar. Looking up at the sky, he watched the raindrops glowing orange in the pale reflected street light, feeling almost dizzy as he followed the lines of the tall office blocks either side of the bar up into the dark night. So quiet. Just a shout, followed by a laugh, from a neighbouring street and the trundle of a dustcart being pushed along the pavement on the main road. The small man lowered his head and inspected his scuffed and dirty shoes. Pulling his jacket shut around his body and tucking in his tie, he stepped purposefully into the rain, the night, the city, thinking of the warm room and hushed conversations he had left behind.

He crossed the alleyway and turned into the main street. The pavement and tarmac shone orange, and the buildings dripped flashes of light. A bus was approaching. No 49. Could get that. No, better to walk. Anyway, I can only get so wet. He strode on, noticing a lone woman passing by on the other side of the road. Her face was obscured by an umbrella but she seemed tall and elegant, dressed in a long coat and high heels. He imagined her as a glamourous femme fatale, going to meet a secret love at a secret location. There are no secret locations, he thought. Only lies.

The small man lowered his head, feeling the water trickle down behind his shirt collar. He was supposed to be going home. She would be waiting, worried. Probably knitting. It's the only thing that calms her down. He chuckled to himself, picturing her in her favourite armchair, a frown across her face and her fingers flicking needles and wool with barely contained anger. I should go home. It'll be warm and dry. There might even be some dinner in the oven. Maybe later. Staying out longer won't make her more angry.

After a while, he reached the cathedral, mesmerised by the glistening beauty of the dome. It's not even that nice a church, taken overall, he mused, but it has presence. You can't beat presence. And then on, through the byways and alleys, away from all sounds and disturbances. The clicking of his shoes echoed off the damp walls. Is someone following? He stopped. The echoes stopped. No point in turning around, just makes you feel worse. He strode on, ignoring the clicking and his paranoia.

Arriving at the next main road, the small man crossed quickly and ducked down another alleyway. He was getting cold. His fingers were white and he could feel the damp through his sleeves and on his back. Should have taken that bus. No. Better not to draw attention. Anyway, can't think on the bus. All that shaking, and stop-starting. No good for my back. He was practically running now. He watched the changing reflections in the water as he raced along the narrow pavement. Round the next corner, and one more to go.

As he reached the entrance, the small man straightened up and tried to shake out his jacket. He placed his tie down the centre of his shirt and pulled out a crease. His hair was damp and matted, but he still flattened it down, tucking the unkempt ends into the top of his shirt collar. He stopped just before the large wooden door and pushed out his round chest, lifting his chin and adopting an imperious expression he had seen in a film the week before. Who was that? Humphrey Bogart? No. James Cagney? Never mind.

He paused before he pushed the bell and breathed deeply. Ring, ring. It sounded so far away. Must be the thick doors. A spy hole shot open and an eye and half a nose appeared. Yes? It's me. Password. Knight to bishop three. The spy hole shut with a bang, and then nothing. The small man shivered slightly, feeling the rain running down his face. Eventually, a bolt slid back and the door opened with a creak. There was a faint glow from within and the small man stepped forward, hearing the door close slowly behind him. As he walked down the dark passageway, he could spot in the dim light words written above the open door in front of him. The Underground Chess Club. The small man smiled and walked straight in.

WATCHING, WAITING

[18 FEBRUARY, 2008]

A DOUBLE ROMANCE

[11 NOVEMBER, 2008]

2 WAS ALONE, SEPARATED FROM THE REST, ON A PART OF THE notepad that was little frequented by other numbers. There weren't even any lines, squares, circles or other regular shapes, and certainly no doodles, to keep the number company.

How the 2 had got there, he wasn't sure. It had happened on a day when a collection of other digits had been called into being in the corner of the notepad nearest to him. Soon after the ink had dried on the page, the 2, with it's slight nick in the top curve and the pressure point at the final part of it's base, had become aware of chattering. 3s, 5s and 8s have always been the more outgoing of the single digits, much to the annoyance of the more recalcitrant 1s and the frankly shy 4s, but it is when they are brought together as pairs that things become a little rowdy, to say the least.

As our 2 started noticing his surroundings, he immediately became aware that there must be a 35 nearby. The chatter and laughter was, well, constant, and not a little irritating to the more peaceful and introspective 2. He also realized that an 18 must have been placed next to the 35, as he could hear a number arguing with itself, insisting that it would like very much talk to the 35 but couldn't quite bring itself to do so.

There seemed to be other numbers in the corner, but the 2 soon became bored with listening to what they were saying, especially as they were too far away to be able to interact with him. The 2 looked around for other shapes and lines in his area of the notepad but soon realised that his part was empty. He could just about make out what must have been a pentagon overlaid with a triangle in the far distance, which was discussing, as far as he could tell, with a squiggle that had two ends, a cloud-like middle and three eyes, the meaning of ink. Being thoughtful and somewhat philosophical, the 2 had no interest in such matters, and turned his attention to a fish and a line of letters in the opposite corner.

The fish, it turned out, was very unhappy with the line of letters, which seemed to spell the word "shark" in capitals. The letters were convinced that they had been written on the page because they went with the fish, because that was the sort of fish that had been drawn. However, the fish argued that he was nothing of the sort. He, as he pointed out in no uncertain terms, looked nothing like a shark. Where was the threatening fin? The tooth-filled mouth? The long, thin body? He was short, round and scaly, with bubbles coming out of his mouth. He couldn't look less like a shark if he had legs and fur. The letters, which can often be aloof and far too literal, were not impressed with the tirade and simply ignored the fish, who continued muttering to himself. Not very edifying, the 2 thought.

As for the rest of the notepad, the 2 could not tell. There seemed to be some sort of shape further down and to the left, and perhaps there was a suggestion of a doodle over to the far right of the page, but he couldn't be sure. One thing was clear, there was nothing close by. And, seeing as he was unable to move, there was nothing he could do but sit and ponder in silence.

Perhaps, it occurred to him after a while, when the rest of the page had seemed to have quietened down a little, another number, letter or shape might be brought into being near him. After all, he had been drawn there. The Ink God had clearly decided that it wanted a number in that space, so it was feasible that it might want another. That would be nice, he thought. Very nice.

He must have drifted off. What seemed like an aeon later, during which the 2 was hardly aware of his own existence and seemed to dream of numbers tangled in lines, falling through endless squares and triangles, there was a sudden commotion. The page was in uproar. The shapes and lines, the numbers and doodles, all were shouting and calling to the space above the notepad. The 2, confused and hardly awake, looked up to see a giant shadow moving across the page.

The Ink God! The figures on the notepad, they could smell the ink from where they lay, trapped in the paper. They were all shouting so that the Ink God would come to them, would call into being another number, letter or shape near to them. They craved the company and the jealously that the others would feel when they realised they had been left out. However, the 2 knew that, all alone, he could never catch the attention of something so mighty as the Ink God. He was too small, and certainly not as pushy as some of the other numbers.

But then, to his surprise, he saw that the shadow had stopped immediately over him. The smell of ink was almost intoxicating, and his head swam as he saw the great Ink Spiller come closer and closer. What would it draw? What would the 2 have for company? There was a crash as the Ink Spiller landed on the notepad, followed by a terrific rumbling as it moved across the surface of paper. The 2 was too shaken and disorientated to know what was going on, but the ordeal was soon over. The Ink Spiller retreated and the shadow moved away. Slowly, hardly daring to look around, the 2 tried to see what had been placed next to him. With a leaping heart, he saw that his greatest wish had been fulfilled. The Ink God had written what is, to the number 2, perhaps the most beautiful and romantic thing it could imagine: 2+2=4.

THE EMPTY ATTIC—A MINI SAGA

[24 JULY, 2008]

ONE DAY, HE CLIMBED THE STAIRS TO HIS DUSTY ATTIC TO HIDE a piece of himself away.

Glowing with pride, every day he concealed another piece from his searching eyes.

Eventually, he forced his entire life into the narrowing space, leaving nothing behind.

The next day, the attic was empty.

THE RAIN

[29 MAY, 2008]

THE RAIN FELL ENDLESSLY TODAY. LONG RIVERS OF WATER tracing over lines in the concrete and tarmac, flowing into metal grates, disappearing into the labyrinth beneath our feet. For a while, I stood at the window of my apartment, staring at the perpetual repetition of drops, the swaying of the leaves on a nearby tree, the smear of grey dragged across the sky. Tiles on a building shining in the dull light. Dark patches on bare brick walls. Cats picking their way across open ground, their sodden fur plastered roughly against their scrawny bodies. Pigeons flapping by in a forlorn attempt to find food, occasionally shaking the water out of their grey-blue feathers. And people, their heads hidden by nylon taut across metal spokes or plastic hoods. Occasionally, someone passed bare-headed, their face held high. I couldn't decide whether they were defiant or wanted to prevent the relentless water running down the back of their neck.

But I soon became tired of the scene. To be honest, I felt as though I was being dragged down with the drops, slammed against the unyielding concrete and swept into the labyrinth. I wanted so much to be happy today. I wanted my thoughts to be picked up on a breeze and carried into the sky, mixing with the pollen and insects, swooping with the twisting, turning birds, floating through the treetops and over the tile mountains. Perhaps I should confess that I haven't been quite as…resolute in recent weeks as I might have hoped.

It is interesting to think how events, occurrences, random or otherwise, can have an impact on one's existence. Take the other day, for example. I had, as my habit dictates, made my usual Wednesday morning visit to the local market to pick up a few vegetables and maybe a treat or two to tide me over until the weekend, and was making steady progress with my swelling bags on my way home. As is also usual, I had to ride out the taunts of the group of young men who gather at the corner of the street next to mine as I made my way home. At first, they didn't seem to say anything in particular that caught my attention. Jibes concerning my threadbare clothes, my unkempt hair, my admittedly unconventional gait and my old-fashioned glasses were aimed at me in quick succession, followed by raucous laughter. I have long-since made myself immune to their comments, especially after Beryl, the woman who sells potatoes at the market, pointed out that they are hardly the most well-turned out young men one could imagine. And so I was immune that day. However, I was surprised when I felt something hit me on the side of the head. The initial shock and sting of the impact was replaced with a sense of dread when I realised that what had hit me was an egg. It was soon followed by another, and then the laughter turned to shouts. I turned slightly to see that the usual gang of young men was larger than normal, with several youths that I did not recognise.

Of course, I should have held my nerve. It is easy to say that now, but I wasn't so…resolute at the time. I started to run, and they ran after me, suddenly quiet, suddenly animalistic. Unfortunately, I have never been fit, and they caught up with me hardly a few yards down my road. I don't even know how it happened, but I was instantly on the floor, kicks raining down on me, sharp pains all over my body. My plastic bags split and could see potatoes rolling across the pavement. At some point, perhaps it was just seconds into their attack, I felt a sharp blow on my head and my glasses snapped and spun away from my face.

And then it was over. There was a shout and the gang scattered, leaving me lying, stupid and lonely, on the floor. Someone helped me to my feet, but I couldn't look at him. A woman tried to put my vegetables back in the bags, but I didn't want them any more. After the people had gone, I just dropped the bags in a bin and went home, back to the only place where I feel comfortable, safe. And, since then, I haven't left these four walls. Every day, I just stand by the window, watching the rain fall endlessly.

EXCERPTS FROM LOST NOVELS

[10 JULY, 2008]

HOPE IS A DECEPTIVE EMOTION. IT IS GRAND, SPACIOUS, ALL-encompassing, and permeates into every aspect of life. Yet, by that very nature, it is a nebulous, elusive concept, and one that disappears as soon as it becomes transformed into reality. That process, of hope becoming reality, is akin to the condensation of a gas into liquid, with all the hot, flowing, penetrating gas that fills up every space in which it occupies deliquescing into a few unprepossessing droplets on the nearest surface. In short, reality is always much smaller and more underwhelming than hope.

Take yesterday, for example. I had, for the past few months, been nurturing, tending, and, some might say, indulging a certain hope, one, I had imagined, would lead on to an almost miraculous turnaround in my fortunes as soon as it was fulfilled. To live intoxicated with such dreams was, in itself, joyous and distracting from the unfortunate nature of the existence that gave rise to my hopes. I had been sustained, even through the greatest privations and most intense humiliations, by my desire, to the extent, I recognise now, that I had lost touch with what could be expected to occur once the gaseous hope that coruscated in my mind had precipitated into an actual experience. It may ever have been thus, yet the crushing reality that resulted was not only utterly devastating but also a complete surprise. As I sit in my barely lit room writing this, I am beginning to wonder if I will ever recover from the disappointment.

Perhaps I should explain. I have been working for the past five years in the civil service in our great capital, presenting myself as best as I can to my superiors and trying to develop some form of comradeship with my colleagues. While I am sure that I am regarded as a reliable, if unspectacular, employee who delivers his work to the specified deadlines and in perfectly acceptable script, I have always floundered when it comes to fostering that other skill necessary in any workplace in order to achieve favour and even preferment: the ability to ingratiate oneself and form bonds with other people. It has occurred to me that I am perhaps seen as something of a loner. What is certain, however, that I am not someone whom other people take into their confidence. I have never been invited out to a meal or a celebration by anyone with whom I work, and any jokes or japes that are shared in our office of fifteen always pass me by, often quite literally. This is particularly galling when our superior, Mikhail Alexandrovich N—, appears from his office to ask what the noise is all about and then joins in, running around the office until the sweat forms upon his brow and he pants with breathless excitement. There have even been occasions when I have become the butt of the jest, and it takes all my self control to be able to sit quietly, still writing without managing to spill a drop of ink, while my colleagues shout and laugh around me, sometimes hitting me on my head with rolled-up papers and trying to knock my arm. Later, I have imagined that I have pushed away from my desk, stood up and rounded on my colleagues, perhaps hitting one with anything that came to hand and cutting down others with quick-witted, expertly timed remarks. After all, they are not without faults, despite their inflated egos. However, such imaginings have remained just that, no matter how many times I have rehearsed them in my mind, alone in my small, dark room.

After many months in despair at my situation and struggling to conjure a solution that would turn me from an often ignored and occasionally ridiculed member of our office into someone with stature and the possibility of advancement, I decided that there was only one way out of my predicament, only one way to show the people who really matter in deciding the course of my career in the civil service, perhaps even my very life in our great capital, that I deserved more. It struck me, after many hours pondering my hopeless situation one cold November evening, when the wind and rain battered relentlessly against my window, that I could do only one thing: I had to meet the head of the civil service in our ministry, Nikanor Ivanovitch F—.

Impossible, I hear you cry. How could someone as lowly as me, Ivan Nikolaevich P—, even think of arranging a meeting with such an august, important and grand individual, a man who makes decisions on the lives of hundreds of thousands of people with a single word, who is the toast of the town, spending night after night travelling from ball to gaming parlour and back again, while dropping in on the Prince for a cosy chat as time permits, and whose very name is the star under which so many people find their guiding light? How indeed, but I can be a determined and stubborn individual when I have set my mind to something, and it became my every wish, felt in every fibre of my being, that I should meet with Nikanor Ivanovitch F—, at which point, I was convinced, he would see my worth, see the value that his ministry should place in me, and lift me to the position I would so clearly deserve.

So it came to pass, just a few short months later, that I stood outside a ballroom in one of the smartest houses in the best part of town, waiting in my best uniform, on which I had spent my last few kopeks in order to ensure that I would look at my best, for a chance to enter and approach the man who would so surely transform my life. It is, of course, a notable reality of life that circumstances never quite turn out as one would imagine and, before I had even a chance to gather my thoughts and check that my hair was straight, I found myself thrust before Nikanor Ivanovitch F— to be offered by the fates my one and only chance in which to bring favour and preferment down upon me. Perhaps the room went silent; I am certain that I cannot remember a single other voice or note struck by the small orchestra while I was in front of my potential benefactor. It seemed therefore as if the attention of the whole world was on me as I stammered out my name, my position in his ministry and that I desired a moment of his time. He seemed so patient, so benevolent, as he asked me to continue. Yet as I started on my speech, I could see the light fade from his eyes and his face set hard, and I inadvertently set myself on a journey that would consume my whole life and have repercussions far beyond my humble existence.

CANDID CAFÉ, ISLINGTON, LONDON

[22 SEPTEMBER, 2008]

THE ELECTRIC LOVE STORY

YES PLEASE!

[10 DECEMBER, 2008]

It was a beautiful day. Sunny. Hardly a cloud in the sky. The sort of day you could fall in love, see a film, roll around in the park, buy a milkshake, help an old lady across the road, fall out of love, drop a magnum into the gutter, find a fiver in your pocket, lose it on the slots, trip over the back wheel of a bike outside the swimming pool, open a bank account and still have time for dinner with your mates. No one would argue with that. Not even them. Mind you, if they did, they were the kind of people you would instantly believe. And make you wish it would start raining.

They. They are h-lo and LA Dave. They are Electric Love. I first met them on a cold Sunday afternoon in 2005, behind the old Magnet bar in Soho. He was dressed in a loud shirt, velvet jacket and skinny jeans. She was sporting an asymmetrical haircut, a pair of shocking grey tights and mini dress that had all heads turning. Neither of them are dressed that way today. They wouldn't. They couldn't. Too much has happened. And that's what they are here to tell me about.

It takes them five minutes to climb the stairs to the small office overlooking Brixton High Street. It isn't my office. I later find out it isn't their office. Later enquiries reveal it isn't anyone's office. They. h-lo and LA Dave. They'd seen it on the internet and rented it out for one day. For the day of the interview. That's the kind of people they are.

As they climb the stairs, they're talking. I can hear them. They sound pleased to see each other. It sounds like months since they last met. Is it months since you last met, I ask them as they walk into the room and look around. He is dressed in a green bomber jacket, Kill the Will t-shirt and low-slung jeans. And a pair of shoes that look as if they have been spliced with a pair of trainers. I later find out they have. Literally. She is wearing nothing. Nothing at all. Apart from a green bomber jacket, Kill the Fill t-shirt and high-slung jeans. And a pair of trainers that... you get the picture. LA Dave looks at h-lo. They both laugh. Out loud. They look at me. He could be the same naïve, trusting, wide-eyed teenager I met back in 2005, apart from the crows feet and the paunch. And the oddly greying hair. She doesn't look a day older than that smile she gave me back then when I asked her about her legion of males fans, including me. That smile. It's 1134 days old. She looks 1134 days older. Maybe more. But they still look like they could fill the dance floor at the flick of a greasy chord.

It's been six weeks, LA Dave says hesitantly. Since we last met. I look puzzled. I had almost forgotten my question. LA Dave looks at h-lo and laughs. They both laugh. I laugh. I don't know why. LA Dave speaks again, slowly, deliberately: I suppose you can say that's months, but it feels more like weeks. LA Dave looks at h-lo. She looks at me. My heart melts, a little. She is still devastatingly beautiful. Yeah, weeks, she says, quietly, sadly, glancing across at the window. I believe her.

But they aren't here to talk about that. Electric Love are here to talk about themselves, their music, the highs, the lows, the in-betweens, the lefts, the rights, the just over theres between up and left that would be called north-west on a compass. You see, it all started so simply. He was a struggling producer, she was a singer with a string of underground hits to her name. The trouble was, they were all so underground that no-one outside her immediate nuclear family had heard of them. But all that was about to change.

One cold January morning on a February evening in March, LA Dave, drunk and stumbling around after another failed project, walked around the corner, a corner just around the corner from the office in which we are currently sitting, and straight into an bleached blonde ingenue. He tripped over his shoe laces and fell at her feet.

Yeah, I remember that! LA Dave thumps the table and stares at h-lo. She cuts in: Yeah, LA kinda lay there for a minute, like he was, like, dead or something. It was, like, totally bosh and I laughed a bit, yeah?

LA laughs and looks back at me: I was totally oblivious of everything. Even my hair. I was that macked.

h-lo laughs: Yeah, you totally were. You were so drunk. It was well bosh. And then, right, he vomited. Right there, in front of my plats. I laughed. I said to him: man, this must be, like, total love. Right here. And LA, although I didn't know his mon then, laughed too, even though he was still macked and vomiting, yeah. Then I, like, looked up. And there, right above me, was this, like, sign. It said Electric Avenue.

h-lo smiles. LA Dave jumps in: Right. And she looked down at me, yeah, still totally macked on the floor, and she said. Hey, it must be Electric Love. And right there and then, I knew we had something.

And so it proved. Over the next six months, they spent hours in the studio, perfecting soon-to-be-legendary dance floor killer faves such as 'Bounce up (bounce back)', 'Push the door (open)', 'Egg plant on my windowsill', 'Will I be in the movies (I suspect not)', and 'Laughing at strangers', all of which formed the core of their groundsealing debut album 'Yes Please!'

What inspired the name, I ask h-lo. She looks nervously at LA Dave and then confidently back at me. LA, like, said yes please a lot when I asked him if he wanted something. It was kinda sweet, so we used it.

And what inspired the sound, that electro-bubble-pop-interstellar-mania feel that was so much a part of your collective identity? LA Dave looks at the floor and knits his fingers. I like chewing gum, sometimes. I like fish fingers and baked beans, sometimes. I like Heat magazine, chick flicks and action movies. Sometimes. Sometimes I don't. Sometimes I like olives, delicately spiced Moroccan food and the work of Kieślowski. Sometimes. But sometimes I don't.

LA Dave pushes his sunglasses up his nose and looks out of the window. I see a bus reflected in the curves of his lenses. I think it's the 159 to Streatham. That bus goes up the hill. But it isn't over the hill. Not yet.

[Read more of our exclusive series on the multi-record selling pop duo Electric Love tomorrow (or the day after, depending on, you know, how things go)]

PLASTIC HEARTBREAK

[11 DECEMBER, 2008]

THE NEXT TIME I SEE h-lo AND LA DAVE WE ARE IN Shoreditch. Well, Hoxton, but you know what I mean. We meet just up from Old Street. In a tiny place off Hoxton Square. I had better not say the name of the impossibly trendy bar where we meet, or it will immediately stop being impossibly trendy and just become trendy. Or worse.

Everyone in there is ultra-bosh, as they might call it, if they aren't too flip-out trendy to use such words. Almost too ultra-bosh, if that's possible. If it is possible, too ultra-bosh would happen there. Right there. Maybe nowhere else. I'll give you an example.

While I'm waiting for them. For h-lo and LA Dave. I see a young kid pop out for a while. He is wearing a sky-blue cardigan, patterned shirt collated from old lumberjack shirts and red jeans so tight he can barely move his legs. He has a mini bobble hat on each finger, a tattoo of Sir Michael Parkinson on his left forearm and a green visor on his head. I think he's running an errand for a studio that makes films for an underground art gallery that no-one has heard of. Literally.

The kid. He is ultra flip-out trendy. Max-ultra-bosh. But when he comes back an hour later, he is no longer fashion forward. Things have moved on. Jeans are baggy now and dark green or mottled pigeon, shirts are stiff and have Edwardian wing collars. And green visors are a joke. A total macked-out joke. And the kid. He knows it, the very first second he walks back in the bar. He cries and runs out. That's how tough things are at the cutting trend-edge.

That was the kind of bar that h-lo and LA Dave walk into 17 minutes and 48 seconds later. I time it. With a replica original Casio watch I wear specially for the occasion. I could never have realised how useful it would be. Neither could h-lo and LA Dave. Oh, them. h-lo and LA Dave. They walk into the bar and everyone stops. They aren't being trendy. They aren't being cool, bosh, anti-mack or whatever you want to call it. They are well above that. They are beyond that. She, h-lo, wears a dress made out of fourteen old doilies sewn together over a white and gold catsuit, with killer heels and a haircut to match. He, LA Dave, wears a pair of Reeboks, a Fruit of the Loom t-shirt and George at Asda jeans. I can't tell who looks more midget-gem-macked-out-ultra-bosh magnet. Neither. It isn't a contest.

They see me and pretend they haven't seen me. I'm used to that. It's part of the ritual. They didn't do it when we met in the office, but then there was no-one to do it for. Apart from me. But I didn't count then, and I am not about to start counting now. Eventually, they come over and slide onto the two stools by the bar I saved for them. Can I get them a drink? Sure, LA Dave says, flicking a tiny badge adorned with the face of Nicholas Parsons onto the bar. Make mine a Kaliber. And h-lo? What will she have? Oh, a Babycham. She sighs and looks out of the window. There is a pigeon, pecking in the dust. That pigeon..., she says, her voice trailing into distance. I know what she means.

But we aren't here to talk about pigeons, or any other birds. We are here to talk about the period in the life of the electro-smash-bubble-pop-sensation that was, and still is, Electric Love, the period that no-one talks about but everyone wants to know about.

After the triumphs of their first album—Yes Please!—and the sell-out European tour, when the world seemed at their feet and practically every teenager on the planet wanted a piece of them, things got difficult for the young duo. LA Dave: Things got difficult for us. LA Dave runs his hands through his hair. Yeah, things got totally macked out, dude-man. h-lo: Yeah. Macked. LA Dave: We didn't know what to do. We got totally scared, I guess. After all the ultra-bosh of the first album came the feeling that, like, well, we couldn't do anything wrong. Like everything we did would be totally perfect bosh.

h-lo drains her glass and orders another drink. She looks at me. Hard. She looks at LA Dave. Soft. And then she looks back at me. h-lo: what I don't get, like, even now, is, like, what actually went wrong. I mean, we totally did the same things, right, used the same boshed-out processes that had worked before. We, like, even wore the same, like, clothes. But nothing we did went right. It was all mack.

LA Dave: right. For 'Yes Please!' I had, like, this totally process that I called vintage jam. Basically, I had this, like, idea that we should only use secondary samples. Samples that had been used before. And we should only cover cover versions. All our music should be second-hand, hand-me-down, vintage. Nothing should be new new. It should be an interpretation of interpretation. Everything should be filtered through someone else's mind, their creative process. It was about making the unoriginal original. You get me?

h-lo: yeah?

I nod, slowly, and then vigourously. This is my way.

LA Dave: well, for this album, right, the second one. You know. 'Plastic Heartbreak'. We did the same thing. But nothing happened. It all just sounded mack.

h-lo: totally.

But the album was still a hit, I insist. The three singles —'Eclectic kettle', 'Sweep my path' and the Beatles-inspired mash-up 'Across the universe (on a plastic love rocket)'— were all mega-dancefloor-smashes. Yeah, they both say, slowly. LA Dave: it did well, yeah. But, for me, and for h-lo… (They look at each other, quickly and then slowly, with a cartoon-effect double-take in between. And then they laugh. Out loud. They look at me, laughing, and I laugh back. I don't know why. Again.) For h-lo too, it wasn't quite the same. It felt as things weren't quite clicking. I think that set the seed for the problems we had with the third album.

h-lo: we were so macked out by all of that, we couldn't, like, even tour.

LA Dave looks at me, and then out of the window. His sunglasses slide down his nose. I can see something glistening in the corner of his eye. I think it's a tear, but it isn't. I never did find out what it was.

[Read the third and final instalment of our exclusive series on the high, lows and in-betweens of Electric Love tomorrow. Or maybe the day after. I am not a machine, you know.]

FEEL ME

[12 DECEMBER, 2008]

IT'S ANOTHER THREE MONTHS BEFORE I SEE H-LO AND LA Dave—the two halves of the electro-bubble-smash-pop-sensation Electric Love—again. Much has happened, both for them and for me. By the time I am riding in a parked taxi halfway along the Old Kent Road at four in the afternoon on bright overcast September morning in late June, I am not sure what, or who, will greet me in the Waz Bar, an achingly trendy joint off the Elephant and Castle roundabout.

I have heard rumours, we all have. Rumours that h-lo has eloped with a Perl programmer from Watford. That LA Dave has opened a sweetshop in Croydon. I even heard a rumour that the Perl programmer had eloped with the sweetshop to the Isle of Skye, but this and many other rumours could not be substantiated. Suffice to say that, at the time of going to press, neither the Perl programmer nor the sweetshop are available for comment, if they ever were.

So, it is with a certain sense of trepidation that I walk into the Waz Bar. I am five minutes late. Normally, I would be at least 45 minutes early in order to soak up the atmosphere and watch them. h-lo and LA Dave. Electric Love to you and me. Walk in the door. However, it took me an hour to realise that the traffic was moving past the window of my taxi, rather than the other way around. And that the driver had abandoned the taxi as soon as I got in.

I order a drink—I don't care what—and grab a seat at a table by the bar. I face the door and wait. They. h-lo and LA Dave. They are late. That much is obvious. I expect nothing less. So, once I have taken a sip of my Blue Nun spritzer, I take in the other customers. It doesn't take long. Aside from a small man in a large coat and even larger hat nursing a drink at the far end of the bar and a young boy in high-waisted trousers, Take That cravat, ring master's tailcoat and bright red trilby sitting near the door, the bar is empty. It's hardly a surprise. Last week, the bar was reviewed by Mind Bender magazine. They told readers they couldn't go. Unless they knew for sure that they were super-bosh-max-flip-out trendy. Not many people have that sort of confidence. Hardly anyone has. Apart from h-lo and LA Dave, of course.

Fifteen minutes and 47 seconds later, they walk in. It's like a nuclear fashion bomb went off in the room. We, all of us, including the stuffed canary behind the bar, look up, amazed. She is wearing electric blue skin-tight PVC trousers, a low-cut frilly long-sleeve white blouse and a luminous yellow scarf around her head, tied like Hilda Ogden. Her bleachblond hair sticks out at the sides. Her shocking red lipstick glistens in the low lighting. She has a six-inch red stiletto on one foot and a flat, grey Converse on the other. She looks almost majestic as she hobbles over to the bar, fifty bangles on each arm clinking with every disjointed, uncomfortable step. He is wearing tight tennis shorts, a giant Blue Harbour fleece from M&S and a pair of beige Hush Puppy loafers. And no socks. She has never looked better. He has never looked worse. Bosh-max-out-flip. Need I say more?

Nine minutes and 12 seconds later, they acknowledge me.

As he slides into his seat, LA Dave flips a bar mat with the face of Michael Crawford circa Phantom of the Opera on one side and a voucher for Chessington World of Adventures on the other into the space between us. h-lo stares right at me. No expression on her face. She is more than devastatingly beautiful. Today. She looks out of the window. Yeah, she whispers. I know what she means. A rubbish truck drives past. Rubbish, she mouths, her lipstick glistening with every move. I believe her.

But we aren't here talk about rubbish. We are here to talk about their—Electric Love's—third album 'Feel Me'. Those are very different things. Very. I ask: So, tell me what happened with the third album? LA Dave glances across at h-lo, scared. She looks away. He looks back at me, brave. LA Dave: Well, you know what, like, happened. It was totally mack. Everyone hated it, even, like, us.

h-lo turns towards me: even us, like.

LA Dave: It was totally hard. Mack hard. Nothing was bosh. Nothing. Me: Didn't you have to abandon your world tour? LA Dave: Yeah, totally. It was our big chance, to max-bosh-out on our success. But it all went mack. Didn't it, h? h-lo: Yeah, he got total antacid addiction after, like, a mild bout of indigestion that wouldn't go. And I had a breakdown after, like, totally missing a fashion show. She looks at the table and pushes her chair back. They both do. It's like they need some space between them and the table. Like it's reminding them of something. I ask them what's wrong. h-lo: there was a table then too.

LA Dave: We tried, like, all sorts of things. Experimented with different genres. We were, like, totally trying to find a new sound. We had to, like, abandon an album of Andalusian nose flute music. It was that mack. After that, I moved to a commune outside Reading. I thought I would find myself, reach a deeper of understanding of myself and the universe that would lift my conscience to a new level. I didn't.

h-lo: You did get crabs, though. Didn't you. When you slept with that ugly tart from Newport.

LA Dave: I thought we said we wouldn't talk about that.

h-lo: Yeah, well, I am talking about it. h-lo looks at me, outraged. She was fat, man. She had a piggy nose, and horrible hair. And all that cellulite. Her legs were, like, disgusting. Totally mack-out ugly. And she was short. Like a midget.

LA Dave: All right, all right. She had a lovely personality, though. LA Dave glances at me for support. I smile non-committedly.

A lovely personality, h-lo says, mockingly. Is that all?

LA Dave: And she made lovely cakes.

h-lo: Lovely cakes? Lovely cakes? You could have eaten the cakes without shacking up with her. Tchh. LA Dave looks sheepish. He fiddles with the zip on his fleece. h-lo looks angry. She picks at a seam on her skin-tight pvc trousers. They glare in opposite directions. I wonder what to say. But then I know what to say. I always know what to say. That's the kind of man I am.

So, what is the future for Electric Love? LA Dave: Well, we just announced some brand new tour dates, and we have booked some time in the studio next week to record new material we have been working on over the past few months.

h-lo: Yeah, and I've been, like, working on some lyrics on my own. Three songs, as a matter of fact. They're called: 'Welsh tart', 'Lovely personality (but have you seen her cellulite?)' and 'Crab-out'. It's all totally drawn from personal experience. h-lo stares at LA Dave and pulls a string of chewing gum out of her mouth. LA Dave looks down and tugs at the zip of his fleece again.

LA Dave. He looks out of the window. His sunglasses are

halfway down his nose. I can see a neon sign across the road reflected in the curve of his lenses. It flashes: Full English Breakfast. It's too late for breakfast. Far too late. LA Dave knows it. h-lo knows it. I know it. But there is always lunch. It's not too late for that. It's a meal. Not the same meal, it could never be that, but it's a meal nonetheless. Sometimes, you have to make do with what you've got.

[That was the last instalment of our exclusive series on the electro-smash-bubble-pop-sensation Electric Love. You can't read any more about them, unless I write some more, of course. It all depends.]

EXCERPTS FROM LOST NOVELS

[27 SEPTEMBER, 2008]

THE SMALL MAN PUSHED BACK FROM THE BENCH AND LIFTED his face to towards the dirty window pane above his head, stretching his back and grimacing slightly as his vertebrae clicked and moved. Yellow light seeped into the room, illuminating the damp in the wall opposite and a pile of rags on the bare stone floor.

A shadow flashed across the window pane. And another. Several in quick succession. And then nothing. The small man listened but could hear nothing save the occasional rumble and faint footsteps rushing on to unknown destinations. He pulled a battered pocket watch from his frayed and threadbare waistcoat and checked the time. A quarter past ten. Four hours. Four hours of copying out sheets of paper. He coughed and looked down at the bench. Piles of paper were arranged on either side of his elbows. One on his left, and two on his right. Still so many left. He wondered how much longer the task would take him and thought about estimating the number of remaining sheets. He soon realised, however, that he would be able to copy out a whole sheet while he attempted his calculation. Instead, he ran a hand over his balding head, tucking in the strands of greasy hair at the back into his yellowing collar. After staring at nothing for a moment, he reached for a small pipe resting in a bowl in front of him and lit it, taking a swift drag before setting it down again and taking up his pen.

Two hours later, the small man laid down his pen and stretched his back again before looking around the room, his eyes readjusting slowly from the inky characters that had filled his eyes all morning. An old chest of drawers stood in one corner, listing slightly on the uneven floor. In the middle of the room lay an old rug, rolled up and half-chewed by mice. In another corner, a broken chair reclined helplessly, a leg snapped in half and another completely missing, the hole in the bottom of the seat like an empty, wooden eye socket. The boy should be here by now, he thought.

Another hour passed. A few more sheets were copied, but far fewer than during the hours of the morning. The small man was feeling uneasy. He picked at a scab on his left forearm and felt under his shirt sleeve. He thought of his wife. After a few moments, he lit his pipe but let it go out before he attempted to take a drag. The shadows flitting by the dirty window pane became more frequent, and the small man took to counting them, wondering if he could detect a pattern in their seemingly random frequency. I should be copying out more sheets, he said out loud. The damp in the walls absorbed the echo, and he felt a shiver run down his spine as it occurred to him that he may never leave the room.

The small man was inspecting the ink stains on his fingers when the lock in the door behind him rattled. The door swung open with a creak. He turned around with a start to see the boy, lolling in the frame, regarding him with a wry grin. You are late, the man said, trying to sound angry. You haven't copied out enough pages, the boy replied. He stepped into the room and lifted a corner of the rug with his boot, dropping it and then stepping over to the bench. Do you know what it says, he said and pulled a sheet from the top of a pile. I might, if I had time to read it, but there are so many sheets. The small man's voice drifted away. I brought you some food. The boy pulled a hunk of bread from within his greasy jacket and dropped it on the bench next to the pipe. The small man gazed at the bread and felt the hunger creeping through him. What about something to drink? This is thirsty work. I'll bring you something in a couple of hours. I have to go now. The boy turned away and walked out of the room, pulling the door shut and rattling the lock into place.

As the room became dark, the small man dragged a small candle towards him and lit it. The flame flickered and jumped, illuminating a small patch of the bench, just enough to see the inky characters and the nib of the pen. The shadows continued to flit by the dirty window pane, but they were nothing more than ghosts in the failing light. The damp patches on the walls waxed and waned in the candlelight, drifting in and out of the darkness. The air lay heavy in the room, the silence broken only by the scratching of the nib on the rough paper and the laboured breathing of the small man. His eyes become tired and his mouth dry. He tilted the jug of beer that the boy had brought, looking for another drop, but there was nothing. He moistened an ink-stained finger to pick up the last of the bread crumbs, prodding the tip into the rough wood. All he could taste was old varnish.

After several hours and having started a new candle, he pulled the pocket watch out of his waistcoat. Half past ten. He lay the pen down and screwed the top back onto the bottle of ink, sliding it into the darkness beyond the candle-light. He pushed back from the bench and pulled a blanket from underneath, unfolding it and laying it down on the floor near the rolled-up rug. Just as he was preparing to lie down and go to sleep, the lock rattled and the door swung open. It was the boy. His wry grin was gone and he had a black eye. He stared at the small man for a moment, gazing at him unsteadily. The small man stood in the middle of the room, holding his waistcoat, which he had just removed, in front of him like a shield. Eventually, the boy spoke. He wants to see you. Now? Yes. He said it was most urgent. What happened to your eye? Never mind about that. You should be more worried about yourself. The small man looked at the blanket on the floor and then his waistcoat. Does he want me to bring the papers? He didn't make mention of them. Do you think I should? I don't care. He just said to fetch you. Now. The small man looked around the room, at the papers and the damp patch. At the chest of drawers and the rolled-up rug. He thought of his wife. I wonder if I shall ever see her again, he thought, and stepped through the open door.

THE BRIDGE—A MINI SAGA

[26 NOVEMBER, 2008]

ON THE BRIDGE, I GRIP COLD GIRDERS WITH BARE TOES. THE water is grey metal, a flowing sheet.

A hand, far away, points. My stomach lurches and my foot slips.

I want to tell you I'm sorry. It was an accident.

But it's too late. Our baby died, after all.

EXCERPTS FROM LOST NOVELS

[25 NOVEMBER, 2008]

I CAN'T SAY I NOTICED. THE OTHER MAN GLANCED DOWN. DID you look? Yes, of course. I mean look properly. Yes, I said so. It's just… What? Just… Just what? Oh, I don't know. It seemed pretty obvious to me.

I'm sorry. I did look. The other man fingered the handle of his cup. I said I'm sorry…look, do you want another coffee? No, I'm okay, thanks.

The two men, who had occupied an outside table at the Maglioni cafe for the past half an hour, looked in opposite directions. One watched locals and tourists at the market picking out fruit and vegetables, while the other followed a line of traffic as it turned at the bottom of the street and away from the cobbled area where they sat. A scooter left the line and came to a wobbly stop on the cobbles. A small man alighted, pulled off his helmet and thrust his keys into the pocket of his shorts. He paused, gazing towards the cafe and the market, and then strode over to an old apartment building, pressing a buzzer and, with a loud click, immediately pushed the door open.

He must have been expected. A pigeon clattered onto the

cobbles between the two men. Who must? The man who went into that block. What block? The man looked away from the market and stared at the back of the other's head. Sorry, I wasn't looking.

Well, there's a surprise. The two men fell silent again and resumed looking in opposite directions.

A waiter came out of the cafe and noisily gathered up the cups and empty sugar packets. Un altro? The man gazing at the market looked emptily at the table and then up at the waiter's apron. He glanced across at the other man, who was staring intently down the street. Si, grazie. The waiter smiled and disappeared back into the cafe. I ordered you a coffee. Yes, I heard. An old woman walked past, dragging a trolley stuffed with vegetables from the market. She stared at the two men and thought of her daughter and son-in-law.

The man in shorts strode quickly out of the apartment block, glancing from side to side. There he is. Who? The man who went into the door. The one I mentioned a minute ago. As the man reached his scooter, he pulled on his helmet and fished in his pocket for the keys. Can you see? It's him. The waiter arrived with new coffees and biscotti. The man who had been gazing at the market nodded in appreciation and turned towards where his friend was looking. He watched the man by the scooter fiddling with something stowed under the seat. Oh, him. Yes, I saw him yesterday.

What? What do you mean? I mean I saw him. Yesterday. When we were in the souvenir shop by the old bridge. I saw him walking past. How can you be so sure? He's wearing a motorcycle helmet. You can't see his face. True, but he hasn't changed his clothes. The two men paused and watched a small, black, plastic object being pulled from of a rucksack under the seat.

Odd place to keep a camera.

It would be, if it was a camera. What is it then? Looks like a timer to me, with something attached to it. The two men turned towards each other.

No, it can't be.

Can't be what? A bomb?

Well, I don't know, but it might be. After all, why else would you have a timer?

If you fancy a boiled egg, if you're making a soufflé.

Very funny. They turned back towards the scooter but it was gone. The man who had been sitting closest to the scooter started in his chair. He stared back at his friend. We should do something. Now.

Do what? Phone the police? What would you say, even if you could explain in your tourist Italian? That a man on a scooter who pricked your overactive imagination is driving around the city with an egg timer?

The man sat back. You said it might be a bomb. As a joke. Christ, you are easy to wind up.

The man closest to the market picked up his cup and lifted it close to his mouth, savouring the smell of the espresso and the perfection of the foam. But, before he could bring it to his lips, a loud bang, like a massive firework, echoed up the cobbled street. It was quickly followed by a bell alarm and a series of screams. He didn't look at his friend. It was too late. He could already hear his shoes clacking across the stones. People were running past. The waiter sprinted out of the cafe and stared at the man as he passed.

The man imagined the plume of smoke before he saw it and felt sick. He'll never forgive me. He whispered out loud, staring at the table. He'll never forgive me. There was no-one in the street now. He looked towards where the scooter had stood and frowned. There it was again. The rider, still with his helmet on, was striding into an office across from the apartment block. The man, still sitting outside the café glanced up and down the street again, his heart beating fast. There was no-one around. Everyone was distracted by the bomb. Of course. That was it. Distracted. The man slowly lifted himself off the metal chair and walked towards the office, pulling his shirt straight. What on earth am I doing? What on earth do I think I'll do when I get there?

Sod it. I have to make up for it somehow. Otherwise, he will never forgive me.

LIVING, GROWING

[28 JULY, 2008]

THE BENCH

[7 NOVEMBER, 2008]

AFTER A WHILE, HE STOPPED COUNTING THE LIGHTS. THERE were too many of them and it was getting cold. So they sat there on the bench at the top of the park in silence, looking down over the town. The wet winter darkness had enveloped the trees and bushes. All that could be seen was the yellow-reflecting clouds. And the lights.

Where's your house, then? A long, slim finger pointed across the valley. The boy tried to follow the line, but it was no use. He couldn't work out which light the finger was pointing to. Where? I can't see. The finger pointed harder, more insistently. There. The boy looked again, but it was impossible. Oh yes, he lied. I see.

Have you been here before?

Where? The park?

No, I mean to see your family.

Oh, no. I haven't. I didn't even know I had family before they wrote. I was just an orphan. They told me there wasn't anyone, just my step-family.

Do you like this lot, then? Your proper family, I mean.

I don't know. They seem all right. Why?

Just wondered. I've sometimes, you know, wondered what it'd be like if a different family turned up and took me away.

Really? Have you?

Sometimes, you know.

Yes, I suppose so.

One of the boys yawned and shivered. A wind blew across the top of the valley. We'd better go back.

I suppose so.

Are you scared?

A bit.

Of what?

That my real family will make me stay here.

Don't you like it here?

No. I mean yes. It's nice. But…

But what?

The thing is, I love my step-family. I'm scared I won't see them again.

Don't worry, they can't make you do something you don't want to.

I suppose not. Can we stay friends, even if I don't stay?

Course.

Thanks, I'd like that.

I SAW YOUR EYES TODAY

I saw your eyes today on a scowled face.
I was on the bus from Brixton to Kennington.
Last week, I caught your smile on a foreign waiter
when I looked up from my drink.

Did you know I spotted your walk
in a crowd of thousands?
It was right in the middle of Oxford Street.
You would have said it was impossible.

Your hand gave me change in the supermarket,
and your hair was on a Hollywood poster
staring down at me from the junction
with Christchurch Road.

And the yellow of your scarf.
It was in a Tube handrail.
I even saw your nose turned up
at the smell of a greasy spoon in Chapel Market.

In a newspaper, I read a joke you sometimes made
and laughed at more than me.
Your feet had blisters
outside a nightclub in King's Cross.

You try every day to make me miss you.
I shan't start now.

ABOUT THE AUTHOR

L.A. Davenport is an Anglo-Irish author and journalist. He has been writing stories, and more, since he was a wee bairn, as his grandpa used to say. Among other things, he likes long walks, typewriters and big cups of tea.

To find out when L.A. Davenport has a new book out, and get the latest updates, visit his official website at Pushing the Wave.

BY L.A. DAVENPORT

FICTION

The Nucleus of Reality, or the Recollections of Thomas P—
Escape
No Way Home
Dear Lucifer and Other Stories
The Marching Band Emporium

NON-FICTION

My Life as a Dog

www.ingramcontent.com/pod-product-compliance
Lightning Source LLC
Chambersburg PA
CBHW070511200726

48293CB00007B/2478